HAZARD

Other books by Michael Senuta:

Incident at Copper Creek
The Vengeance Brand
Matt Train
The Hidden Truth

HAZARD

•

Michael Senuta

AVALON BOOKS
NEW YORK

Published by Avalon Books,
an imprint of Thomas Bouregy & Co., Inc.
160 Madison Avenue, New York, NY 10016

Library of Congress Cataloging-in-Publication Data

Senuta, Michael.
  Hazard / Michael Senuta.
      p. cm.
    ISBN 978-0-8034-7799-5 (acid-free paper)
1. Historians—Crimes against—Fiction.   2. Private
investigators—California—Los Angeles—Fiction.
3. Murder—Investigation—Fiction.   I. Title.
  PS3569.E63H39 2010
  813'.54—dc22
                                        2010020481

PRINTED IN THE UNITED STATES OF AMERICA
ON ACID-FREE PAPER
BY HADDON CRAFTSMEN, BLOOMSBURG, PENNSYLVANIA

To my parents,
William and Cathyrnne

Chapter One

For the last fifteen years, the sign on my office door has read DOYLE & HAZARD. Even though my partner, Charlie Doyle, retired five years ago, I decided not to change the name of the agency. As a private-investigating firm, we were at one time considered top of the line; however, changes in technology, larger organizations, and society's needs in general relegated us to a making-a-living status as opposed to enjoying a lucrative existence. The profession had lost its glamour for me, and, to tell the truth, I had become a bit jaded. According to my accountant, if I managed to hold on for another three years, I could retire in comparative comfort. Therefore, I continued to plod along.

It was Friday morning, and I was buried in paperwork from my last case when my secretary, Leigh Masters, entered my office. I could always tell Leigh's mood by the way she walked. Today, she was deliberate and businesslike as her high heels clicked quickly on the floor as she approached my desk.

1

"Boss, I've got trouble. I'm going to have to leave for a while."

I glanced up and considered her. She was pale, her usually big brown eyes were narrow, and her lips were compressed. "What's wrong?"

"I got a call from home. My mother's had an accident. She was taken to the hospital," she returned, an obvious edge in her voice.

"I'm sorry, kid. Any word on her condition?"

She shrugged.

"Your mother lives in San Luis Obispo, doesn't she?"

"Yes."

"That's a couple of hours. Do you want me to drive you?"

"No thanks. I think I'd rather be by myself. Focusing on driving will help keep my mind off my worries."

"Sure. Take the rest of the day. For that matter, take Monday if you need to."

"Thanks, boss." She wrung her hands as she stood in front of me, shifting her weight uneasily from one leg to the other. "I made coffee, and I opened the mail. There's nothing urgent."

"Forget all that. Just go. I'll see to the office."

She nodded and then turned on her heels and left.

I thought about her for a long time after she was gone. She was a highly efficient secretary and a genuinely decent person. She was also very close to her mother. I figured Mrs. Masters must be about sixty-five. I had a pretty good idea what Leigh was going through right now. I continued to work, although my attention was fragmented as thoughts of Leigh ran through my mind. I was almost glad when the telephone rang.

"John Hazard," I announced as I picked up the receiver.

"Mr. Hazard, this is Darrin Thomas," the voice said. "I'm personal secretary to Richard Armitage."

The name immediately struck a chord. "Armitage . . . the writer?"

"That's correct. He was wondering if you would be available for a brief interview this afternoon—say, about two o'clock?"

"Yes, that would be convenient."

He provided me with an address, which I jotted on my notepad.

I hung up the receiver and stared out the window for a long moment. The name Richard Armitage piqued my interest. I had read and admired his work for years. Although he had penned an occasional novel, he was primarily a historian, having written extensively about California and Nevada. His works had earned many awards. I wondered exactly what such a man as Armitage would want with a private investigator.

I finished most of my paperwork, checked my watch, and decided I had time for lunch before my appointment. I placed some forms in a manila folder, scribbled a few instructions for Leigh, and dropped the bundle on her desk on my way out.

I generally had lunch at the diner across the street

whenever I was in or near my office at the noon hour. It was run by an old Marine Corps buddy of mine named Barney Kennedy. About seven years ago, I had gotten him out of a jam and helped him get started in his business. He had done all right for himself ever since. He also made the best bowl of chili I'd ever tasted.

The diner was called Barney's Eatery. It was of chrome construction, stylized in the fashion of the typical roadside oasis you used to see so often on Route 66. What set Barney's place apart from the run-of-the-mill establishment was that it was immaculate. From its spotless windows to its shiny red vinyl booths to its sparkling silverware, Barney's place epitomized the word *clean.*

I entered through the side door and slid into the nearest booth—the one I always preferred if it was unoccupied. I noticed a few of the regulars at the counter, sipping their coffee or reading their newspapers. We exchanged greetings, and I picked up a menu.

Margie, Barney's only full-time waitress, immediately stepped over and placed a steaming cup of coffee in front of me. "Hi, John," she said, welcoming me with a friendly smile. She was about forty, with dark curly hair that hung in short bangs over her forehead. She had a pretty face with a figure to match. It was no secret that she had a thing for Barney, but Barney did not seem to be the marrying kind. Even so, Margie came to work every day, rain or shine, and worshipped her boss from afar, but she never made him uneasy about her feelings toward him.

"Hello, Margie. You're looking radiant today."

"Thanks." She glanced over her shoulder toward the kitchen window. "It's nice that *someone* thinks so."

"Patience, Margie. Everything will fall into place."

"Uh-huh."

"How's the roast beef today?"

"Tender."

"All right, I'll have a sandwich with a trace of mayo. Put some lettuce and tomato on the side."

"You've got it." She turned and walked behind the counter, where she called out the order to Barney.

A minute later, Barney emerged from the kitchen. He was about forty-five, with the build of a linebacker. His face was full, and he still wore his hair in a flattop, just as be did when I had first met him at El Toro. "Whaddya say, Haz?" he asked as he adjusted his long white apron.

"Hello, Barney."

"No chili today?"

"No, I'm not in the chili mood."

"Suit yourself. I've always got a pot going. You on a case?"

"I've got a meeting this afternoon. It might lead to something. It's too early to say."

"Good. I know things have been slow for you lately. How many more days before you reach the big *R*?"

"Roughly three years and ten days. I'll be fifty-five,

and, financially secure or not, I'll dust off my fishing pole and head for the nearest pier."

"Let me know. I'll go with you."

I nodded.

"Your roast beef will be up in a few minutes. You want some mashed spuds with it? I just made brown gravy."

"No thanks. I'm traveling light today."

"Okay, pal."

A few minutes later, Lou Kaiser sidled into the diner. He patted a couple of the patrons on the back, exchanged some friendly banter with them, and then spotted me. Grinning, he stepped over to my booth and slid into the seat across from me. Lou carried 130 pounds on his five-ten frame. His pencil-thin mustache and long, aquiline nose gave him a weather-vanelike appearance. There was no "angle" that Lou had not yet explored.

"Hi, Hazard."

"How are you, Lou?"

He shrugged. "Still lookin' for the winner's circle."

"Tell me about it."

Margie brought my meal and refilled my cup. "Hello, Lou. You want something?" she asked as she patted Lou on the shoulder.

"Just a coffee to go, Margie."

She nodded and retreated to the counter.

Leaning over the table, Lou said, "You couldn't spare a sawbuck, could you, Hazard? I've got a sure thing in the fourth at Santa Anita."

"Oh, yeah? What's his name?"

"Robin's Arrow."

"Robin's Arrow?"

"He's hot. He doesn't look like much, but when the flag goes down, he's the one to beat. Won his last two races."

I took a bite out of my sandwich. The roast beef all but melted in my mouth.

"The trainer's a friend of mine. Says this is the best pony he's ever handled."

I reached into my pocket and pulled out a twenty. "Put a sawbuck on him for me too."

Lou smiled. "Thanks, Hazard. You won't regret it," he said, picking the bill out of my hand and slipping it into his shirt pocket.

Margie returned and set a Styrofoam cup in front of him. "Shall I put it on your tab?"

"Yeah, sure, Margie." He smiled as he slid out of the booth.

Margie stood with one hand on her hip while she held the coffeepot in her other. "You know, in all the time I've known Lou, I can never remember his leaving the same way he came in."

I shrugged. "He's cautious."

"I guess so. How's the sandwich?"

"It's probably the best roast beef I've ever had."

"I'll be sure to tell Barney."

I nodded as I plowed into the rest of the sandwich. The combination of the beef and the side salad hit the mark. I ate it with pleasure, paused for a moment as I reflected how good it actually was, and then drained the coffee from my cup. A few minutes later, Margie gave me a refill, and I finished that as well, although I lingered over my last cup a bit longer. I left some money on the table, along with a five for Margie, and then headed for my car.

The address that Richard Armitage's secretary had given me was in Santa Monica. Although I had not been there for some time, several of my former cases had taken me there, and I was familiar with the community. In fact, when I was a kid, my family's favorite restaurant was located there; now, though long gone, the spot held fond memories for me.

I drove down a shady, tree-lined street that boasted a number of stately residences quietly adorned with neatly pruned shrubbery and beds of colorful flowers. Armitage lived in an imposing three-story Victorian that, despite a bit of deterioration, still reflected the elegance and refinement that characterized so many sections of the city. I parked at the curb and made my way up a long sidewalk, still damp from a lawn sprinkler nearby. I climbed two stone steps and rang the doorbell. After a short wait, the door opened, and I stood facing a man of about forty, with thick black hair, wire-rimmed glasses, and a dark mustache.

"Mr. Hazard?"

I nodded.

"I'm Darrin Thomas. We spoke on the phone this morning. Please come in."

I entered the house and found myself in a roomy foyer. The ceiling was high, and a crystal chandelier hung from somewhere in the shadows above. The wallpaper was an understated earth tone in color, and the furniture was heavy looking and highly burnished. A parquet floor gleamed against the light cast by the hanging fixture.

"Come this way, Mr. Hazard. Mr. Armitage is working in the library."

I noticed that Thomas limped a bit as I followed him down a short corridor that led to a large but dimly lit room. The only source of light was a single lamp with a green shade that was placed on a long table. It took a moment for my eyes to adjust, but when they did, I saw row upon row of shelves on every wall lined with what must have been thousands of books.

"Thank you for coming, Mr. Hazard."

I focused my eyes on a man who was seated next to the table. He wore a light-colored tweed sports coat and a green cravat. His legs and lap were covered with a blanket. He appeared to be about eighty, with a head of thick gray hair, a coarse but well-groomed mustache, and a rather prominent nose.

"I'm Richard Armitage," he announced as he moved closer.

It took a second for me to realize that he was in a wheelchair.

Thomas moved behind him and stood near the bookshelves.

"How do you do, sir? I've read many of your books. It's a great honor."

His expression reflected a deep appreciation for my remark. "You're very kind," he said modestly as he shook my hand. His grip was firmer than I expected for someone of his age, and his voice seemed that of a younger, more active man. "Please sit down," he said, directing me toward an armchair.

As I sat, I noticed a number of papers strewn across the table as well as several books—some open, some closed but marked with strips of paper.

Noticing my glance, Armitage said, "As you, no doubt, have divined, I'm working on my latest book."

"That's good news. I'm sure your legion of readers will be delighted to hear it."

He smiled. "I'll come directly to the point, Mr. Hazard. Although we've never met, your firm was recommended to me by an old friend who once had dealings with your former partner. I don't really need a private investigator in the conventional sense. In fact, you may consider my proposal out of your line. If so, feel free to turn it down."

I sat back and listened intently.

"What I really need is someone who is trustworthy and dependable, someone who can do a job for me that I am no longer able to do myself."

"Go on, Mr. Armitage."

"I've been doing some historical research on our state with a concentration on the latter half of the nineteenth century. My studies have taken me in many directions. Recently, I discovered a fascinating town called Silver Butte."

"Silver Butte . . . I've never heard of it."

He smiled. "That's not surprising, because it no longer exists. That is, no one lives there anymore." He must have sensed my confusion, because he continued. "It's a ghost town."

"A ghost town?"

"That's right. I recently learned that one of my ancestors once lived there. In fact, it's entirely possible that he might even have been one of its founding fathers. The history of such communities as Silver Butte is often lost. What we do know is this: a rich vein of silver was discovered at the base of a huge butte—hence, the name of the town. A shaft was dug, and before long, an industry was begun in the desert . . . in the middle of nowhere— mining. Along with that discovery came hundreds, then thousands of silver-seekers hoping to make their fortunes. With them came others who saw an opportunity to make money by providing the miners with basic needs. General stores, livery stables, freight offices, restaurants, saloons, hotels, boardinghouses sprang up virtually overnight. It's a familiar story. There were many such towns that sprouted up throughout the West, and many of them suffered the same fate. When the mines played out—and they did—there was no longer any reason to stay on. We know about the depletion of the silver, but there are other stories connected with Silver Butte that we can't authenticate. For example, at least one document hinted at a cholera epidemic. Still another tells of an Indian raid. So far, my research has been sketchy . . . incomplete. I need more data . . . hard evidence to support my writing and bolster my theories. I'd like you to go there . . . to Silver Butte. I'd like you to institute a search for anything that might provide me with information concerning the history of the town. Legal documents, letters, bank statements, deeds, land-office records, hotel registers—even something that may seem trivial might prove to be extremely enlightening to me."

Hearing him speak was almost like reading an account from one of his histories. I was mesmerized by his deep, sonorous voice and the clarity of his sentences. "Do you think such documents still exist?"

He shrugged. "Perhaps, perhaps not, but the desert has ways of preserving the past. Sometimes one finds a diamond among the ashes."

I considered his proposal with interest. "I've been a private investigator for better than fifteen years, but I do believe that this is the most unusual request anyone has ever made of me."

"I realize that it is a bit unorthodox. I'd go myself, but I've been in this chair for some time now, and I can't spare Darrin at the moment. I can't imagine that this job should occupy you for more than a few days, once you get to Silver Butte. I'll pay whatever fee you consider reasonable and whatever expenses you incur, of course. There's no danger involved, but you might have to rough it for a while, and you'll certainly get your hands dirty."

"It's an interesting proposition. I'd consider it an honor just to be associated with Richard Armitage and his work."

He beamed. "Very good. Darrin, give Mr. Hazard the map and point out the location of our once-prosperous community."

Darrin picked up a map from the table and spread it under the lamp.

I moved to the table and studied the area that was marked out.

"This is probably your best route from Los Angeles," Darrin indicated, tracing an index finger along the map. "You'll leave the main highway at this point and take this secondary road that I marked. You'll drive for approximately fifteen miles before you leave that and head northeast. Another ten miles or so should place you in downtown Silver Butte. Here, I've marked it with an *X*."

I nodded. "It seems straightforward enough."

"You'll be traveling across some pretty rough desert terrain once you leave the secondary road. It might be more convenient for you if you were to camp out in Silver Butte."

"I do some camping on occasion. I have the equipment."

"Splendid! When do you think you can leave, Mr. Hazard?" Armitage asked.

"Well, I just concluded a case a few days ago. The paperwork can wait. I'm free at the moment. I suppose I can start Monday."

"Could you start tomorrow?"

"If it's that important to you, I imagine I can."

Armitage seemed relieved at my answer. "I'm delighted to hear you say that. Forgive me for appearing so anxious, but I am in a bit of a rush to finish my research. You see, this will be my last book."

I eyed him in surprise.

"I've been ill for some time now, and my doctors have not been generous with their prognosis. Oh, I have a good six months yet—maybe even a year—but they have cautioned me to cut back on my work. They're right, I suppose. I tire easily now, and the energy needed to complete a book is beyond that which I can muster nowadays."

"I'm sorry to hear that."

"Don't harbor any regrets. I've lived a long, productive life."

"Your books will serve as your legacy for many generations to come."

"Thank you," he replied, obviously deeply pleased by the compliment.

"When I return, how would you like me to contact you?" I asked.

"You can reach Mr. Armitage at this number," Thomas said, handing me a card.

"All right. I hope I can find something of use to you, Mr. Armitage."

He extended his hand, and I took it.

As I left Santa Monica behind, I replayed all of the details of my meeting with Richard Armitage. He was an interesting man, and I could not help but feel a personal sadness in knowing that his days were numbered. I was proud that he had chosen me to undertake this phase of his research—perhaps the last phase. At least I would be able to contribute in some small measure to his final work. I would be sure to request an autographed copy of the book.

I turned on the radio to help pass the time while I was waiting for a traffic jam to clear. The newscaster, I thought, sounded a little like Armitage except that his voice lacked the rich resonance of the writer's. Although I had never seen Armitage before, there was something in his voice that was vaguely familiar to me. Perhaps I had heard him speak on the radio at some time in the past. The traffic started to move again, and I shifted my attention to other matters.

I decided to return to my office to see if Leigh had called. On the way, I stopped at a dealership run by a friend of mine, Jerry Dodge, and arranged to borrow an all-terrain jeep. Then I went into a supermarket and bought some lunch meat, a bag of ice, and some bottled water. I never drank bottled water, but for my excursion tomorrow, I thought it might come in handy.

It was nearly five before I unlocked my office door. I stepped over to Leigh's desk and turned on the answering machine. There had been no calls. I began to worry. She should have telephoned by now to let me know about her mother's condition. I knew that Leigh kept her mother's number on file in case I needed to reach her there. Flipping through her Rolodex, I quickly found it and dialed the number. It was busy. I jotted down the number on a notepad and tore off the paper. I would try her again as soon as I got home.

My apartment was nothing extravagant, but it was presentable and comfortable. More than that, it suited my personal needs. I had a nice kitchen, a spacious living room, a bath and a half, and two bedrooms, one of which I had converted into a den with a sleeper sofa and enough shelf space for a few hundred books. The apartment had been my home for the last ten years. I had a good relationship with the landlord—an ex-client of mine who had been so grateful for my services that he charged me at least two hundred a month less than he could have gotten on the open market.

After stowing my groceries, I tried Leigh again. This time, following half a dozen rings, she answered the phone.

"Leigh, it's John. Is everything all right?"

"Everything's fine. Mother is okay. There was no accident. It was all just a bad mistake."

"What do you mean?"

"Well, I don't know exactly. The first thing I did when I got here was go directly to the hospital. No one there knew anything about Mother's being in an accident. According to their records, no one from the hospital called me. I don't know whether it was just some kind of a mix-up or someone playing a sick joke."

"Is your mother there with you now?"

"Yes. After I left the hospital, I came directly to her house. Unfortunately, she wasn't here. I would have telephoned you earlier, but I didn't know where she was. I didn't know if she was all right. I was still worried. I called on some of her neighbors, but they knew nothing about any accident either. It was some time before Mother came in. She had been out shopping. She was surprised to see me, and she was stunned by my story. I'm afraid she's a little shaken by all of this."

"Well, whatever happened, at least she's all right."

I could hear Leigh taking a deep breath and slowly releasing it into the receiver.

"Leigh, stay with her. Make a long weekend of it. Take Monday if you need it as well."

"I couldn't do that. I'm sorry I had to leave at all."

"Don't sweat it."

"I can drive back tomorrow and finish the paperwork on the Randall case."

"No, no. That can wait. Something new has come up, and I'll be out of town for a few days."

"Oh?"

"It's an unusual case. I'll explain everything when you get back."

"But, boss—"

"Don't worry. The paperwork will be here when you return. Just relax . . . and give Mrs. Masters my best."

"Thanks, boss. I will."

My camping gear was packed away in one of my closets. I removed everything and selected those items I thought I would need. These, I checked carefully. I had a large leather valise that I sometimes used when I traveled. I removed it from its shelf, thinking that it would serve well as a container for any documents I might find at Silver Butte. I also located my compass and packed a notebook.

I then took some denims and work shirts from my closet, along with my trail boots and a pair of work gloves. Satisfied, I replaced the articles I would not be taking. Finally, I aligned all of my equipment on my living room floor in the order I wanted to pack it in the morning.

I cooked a steak for dinner and ate it off a tray in my den while I watched the evening news. I studied the map again that Darrin Thomas had given me while I had my third cup of coffee.

I showered and set my alarm for six-thirty. I located

one of my books authored by Richard Armitage and read for about an hour before I decided to turn in. My impression of his talent was, once again, reinforced. Just before I fell asleep, I thought about the strange day that Leigh had had. She had obviously been unhinged by it all. She was a good girl, and I hated to see her so upset. Leigh was the last thing on my mind before I fell asleep.

Chapter Two

The following morning, after a breakfast of bacon, eggs, and toast, I took delivery of the jeep Jerry had arranged for me to use on the previous day. The teenager who drove it over was elated when I slipped him a ten. I then skimmed the morning paper while I finished my coffee. Next, I loaded the ice chest with the items I'd purchased the day before. I also threw in a couple of steaks from my freezer. I put some canned goods into a paper bag and then began packing the equipment into the jeep. I rolled up my .38 into my sleeping bag and put on my Dodgers cap. It was shortly after eight-thirty when I hit the road. I knew I was going into the heat of the desert and mountains, but I looked at it as a pleasant change from the traffic and smog of the city. Besides, I might benefit from some fresh air and a little isolation.

The traffic seemed reasonably light for a Saturday morning, and I made good time as I left the city streets behind and passed through the outskirts of Los Angeles. It was a cheerful day. The sun was bright with only a few drifting clouds high in a blue sky. I picked up Interstate 15 and headed north-northwest. In time, I passed Apple Valley, Victorville, and soon left Barstow in my rearview mirror. I had made this drive before, several times, when I vacationed in or had business in Las Vegas. It all looked pretty much the same to me except for maybe a few more convenience stores here and there.

The land opened up, with vast expanses of sand and sage. I had always liked the desert—the great vistas, the constantly changing contour of the land. I marveled at the mountains in the distance, sharply contrasting with the rest of the horizon. The land on both sides of the highway was dotted with cactus, clusters of rocks, and an occasional roadside sign that served to remind the traveler that he was in the twenty-first century. Once in a while a huge jackrabbit would dart across the pavement, only to disappear into the underbrush just yards away from the wheels of the jeep.

Not many cars passed me during my drive. In fact, there were long periods when I saw no one in the distance or in my rearview mirror. It was a different kind of feeling, being completely alone with so much space around me—especially since I was a city dweller accustomed to crowds, traffic, and noise—but it was a good feeling. During one lonely stretch I watched a hawk circling in the air currents high overhead. I observed him as he glided effortlessly, rarely flapping his wings yet still maintaining his elevation. For the moment, it was as though we were the only two living creatures on earth.

The heat waves dancing on the pavement ahead reminded me that I was getting hot. I turned on the air conditioner, and in no time at all, I felt more comfortable and enjoyed the drive that much more.

I soon reached the point on my map where I had been directed to leave the Interstate for a dirt road that took me even farther from civilization. From here on, the going was rougher as I churned up a long trail of dust that swirled behind me before it finally settled again, leaving no trace of my passing except for some transient tread marks in the sand. I slowed my speed to accommodate the terrain and checked my odometer frequently in order to be ready for my final turnoff. Although the land did not advertise any obvious change in elevation, I sensed a gradual incline.

When, according to my odometer, I was due to change direction, I stopped the jeep and assessed my position. I stepped outside and strolled away from the vehicle. The hot, dry air immediately struck me, and despite a slight breeze, I felt little relief against the harshness of the desert. As I stretched my legs, I scanned the lay of the land I had just traveled. Except for a few small rises that lent sparse moderation, there was an unbroken span of desert stretching all the way to the horizon. Ahead were rocky outcroppings that broke through the earth like splinters from a giant block of wood, more vividly defined inclines, and even sharper peaks farther in the distance. I pulled out my compass and determined my future course. One prominent tor, in particular, caught my eye. It lay on an almost exact northeasterly path. How far away it was, I could not determine. Distances in the desert were deceiving, but I estimated it at approximately five or six miles. Once I reached it, I knew I would be very close to my destination.

I made my way back to the jeep and removed a bottle of water from the ice chest. I took several swallows. It went down smoothly, and I immediately felt refreshed. I got behind the wheel and restarted the engine. The cold air came on again, and I sat there for a few minutes enjoying it and thinking how much modern-day travel beat a covered wagon. I put the jeep into drive and moved on.

It turned out that the rocky tor was not five or six miles away. It was eight. From its base, I spotted what appeared to be a black streak in the distance. As I drove, the black streak became more defined, and I knew that I was looking at what could only be the town of Silver Butte. I grew excited as I approached it, increasing my speed now that I realized I had reached my destination. The outlines of the buildings against the sky now loomed close enough to give me a more distinct impression of the layout of the town. My initial impression was that there was one main thoroughfare that intersected on the north end with another, shorter street. One large building, flanked by a long corral, stood on the south end of the main street—probably a barn or livery. I pulled the jeep up to the main street and parked at the south end. I killed the ignition and climbed out. Again, the hot, dry air struck me, and I instantly missed the air conditioner of the jeep.

The first thing I decided to do was to walk through the town to get a more accurate perception of its dimensions and to determine the number of individual structures. This would give me a better indication of how to go about my exploration. I also thought it might be useful to Mr. Armitage if I were to sketch a diagram, charting each building and noting exactly where I found any documents or items of interest.

The largest building was, as I had surmised, a livery stable. There was a sign over the door indicating as much, but most of the letters had long since faded. Walking down the main street, I counted some half a dozen buildings on either side, all but a few of them one-story. A warped boardwalk stretched in front of each building, and hitching posts ran practically the length of the entire street. When I reached the only intersection, I saw more of the same, running east and west. At a glance, some of the structures appeared sturdy enough, while others were questionable. One building was nothing but a shell, its roof caved in and its walls charred black. I could only guess what business might have existed here and if anyone had perished in whatever disaster had befallen it.

Looking up a slight gradient toward the east, I could make out the opening of a shaft in the side of the butte around which the town had been built. Timbers, piles of rocks, and old carts were strewn all over the ground, abandoned like so many toys that had been left behind by oversized children. Several outbuildings also dotted the landscape, some of which had collapsed into piles of boards and tar-papered roofs, leaving nothing behind as to what significance they might have held.

A hint of a breeze failed to allay the sweltering heat, managing only to blow dust across the street and create the usual sounds one could expect to hear in an old, deserted town—a loose shutter tapping against a wall, a warped door squeaking as it dangled from its hinges. It was an interesting location. It reminded me of Knott's Berry Farm, where my parents often took me as a child. At any moment, I expected to see Clint Walker or Chuck Connors riding down the street and dismounting in front of me.

I smiled to myself as I walked back to the jeep. It had been a long ride and a while since I had eaten, and I decided that I was hungry. I took some bread from the grocery bag and selected three slices of salami from the ice chest. I sat on the boardwalk in front of the nearest building and enjoyed my sandwich as I contemplated the town of Silver Butte. I thought it strange that, little over a century ago, it had been a beehive of activity, and today there was not even one soul left to relate the town's history. Armitage was right. Silver Butte was like so many other communities to suffer the same fate. As the silver disappeared, so did the people. I washed down my sandwich with some bottled water and resolved to go to work. I secured the valise, my notebook, and my work gloves from the jeep. I decided to start with the first building on the main street and systematically move up the block.

The first structure had no sign over the doorway, nor was there a door. The boardwalk creaked beneath me as I stepped onto it. Gingerly, I entered. At six-foot-two and two hundred pounds, I wanted to make certain I did not crash through rotten flooring and end up with a sprained knee or a broken ankle. To my left was a long counter layered with dust. The floor was carpeted with sand, more so in the corners than in the center—an accumulation of what must have been a good many years. Meandering tracks of lizards and small rodents decorated the floorboards. I walked around but found nothing of interest. A few papers were pinned to one wall, but they were so faded, they were illegible. The shelves behind the counter yielded nothing, and the back room was empty save for a broken barrel and a wood bin. I could scratch one building in Silver Butte.

The next structure had a sign over the door that read FREIGHT OFFICE, and at least, it had a door. I struggled with it and was ready to throw my shoulder against it when it finally yielded to my efforts. Inside, I found more of the same—emptiness, sand, and dust. A back door opened to a small corral with a water trough half-filled with sand. Strike two.

The next building was a barbershop, but there was nothing left of any significance—not even a barber's pole or a chair. Everything had been stripped clean except for a wall mirror and some empty bottles on a shelf. A few had labels, but they were too faded to read.

I was beginning to think that my venture was going to be a complete waste of time until I entered the next building—the mercantile. It, too, had been pretty much picked clean. There were no tools—they would have been valuable commodities, unlikely to have been left behind. There were, however, some bolts of cloth, now long since faded and dust covered. Some catalogues remained on one of the counters. I thumbed through one of them and marveled at the items and their prices. According to the inside covers, they had been published in Philadelphia. Next to the catalogues, I found two pieces of paper with writing on them. At first glance, they appeared to be indecipherable, but upon closer examination, I found that I was able to read them. They seemed to be grocery lists, with such items as flour, sugar, coffee, and the like on them. One had the name J. Carter; the other A. Randolph. Quite possibly I had come across the names of two residents of Silver Butte. I carefully placed the lists and the catalogues into my valise, recorded my find, and resumed my search.

The next building was a saloon. The bat-wing doors were still in place, although one dangled by a hinge. I sidled inside and found a large chandelier covered with cobwebs suspended from the ceiling in the middle of the room. Only a few wooden tables and chairs remained of what must have been one of the most popular gathering places in the community. A long bar with a cracked mirror behind it lined almost the entire length of one wall. I could see my dim reflection as I crossed the room, and I wondered how many gunfights might have occurred on this very spot. Behind the bar I found some empty bottles, a few kegs, and several empty crates. The back rooms yielded little more than a wooden mallet and a broken Colt .45. I passed through the back door and discovered still more crates loaded with empties neatly stacked against the rear of the building.

Crossing to the opposite side of the street, I decided to visit next the Silver Butte Hotel, where I hoped to have better luck. My impression was that the hotel was the largest structure in town except for the livery. The foyer was sizeable, with a divan and some thickly padded armchairs scattered about. They were frayed and, like everything else I found, layered with dust. I had hoped to find a hotel register behind the reservation desk, but there was none. Off the foyer was a dining room, which must have been reasonably elegant, considering the era. A few tables and chairs had been left behind. I walked through the dining room and into a kitchen, which seemed well equipped with nice cupboards—now completely empty—and a long butcher table. Next to the back door was a sink with a pump layered with cobwebs. I tried the door, but it failed to respond. When I applied force, the doorknob came off in my hand. For the time being, I decided to abandon the rear of the hotel and retraced my steps through the dining room and into the foyer again. I considered the staircase leading to the second floor. The outer banister was missing, and the steps looked rickety. I had second thoughts about contending with it, but I decided to give it a go, keeping close to the wall as I climbed. When one of the stairs started to give under my weight, I stepped up over it and, with caution, made it to the second-floor landing. Methodically, I went from one room to the next, canvassing each with care. Every room had been stripped of its furnishings but one, where a bed frame and some springs had been left behind. In the closet of another room, I found a tattered coat hanging from a hook and a carpetbag with some remnants of clothes, but nothing more.

Next to the hotel was the bank, where only the tellers' cages remained. Here, I found some blank withdrawal slips and some stationery with the bank's letterhead on it. There was no furniture at all. Even the vault had been packed up and hauled away. I took samples of everything.

The sheriff's office proved to be more rewarding. Here, I found half a dozen WANTED posters tacked to a bulletin board. There were no pictures, only names and descriptions of outlaws and amounts offered for their capture. These, I carefully filed away. There was a small desk off in one corner. Inside one of the drawers was a log containing what appeared to be a list of prisoners, their crimes, and the dates they had spent behind bars. There were a few dozen names over a period that covered some six months—a good indication, perhaps, of how long there had been a peace officer in Silver Butte. I hoped to discover a famous desperado like Johnny Ringo or John Wesley Hardin, but I did not recognize a single name in the lot. The interior room contained a pair of cells with bunks. The blankets, mattresses, and springs were gone—only the frames remained. I took the log and the posters with me and moved on. One of the town's eateries—Mary's Cafe—flanked the jailhouse. It, too, had been cleaned out. Except for a broken chair and a crate of shattered crockery, there was little left. I did pick up an interesting menu from the counter. Stew was advertised for 75¢, coffee was 10¢, and eggs went for 15¢. Such steep prices so long ago made me conclude that most residents of Silver Butte were doing quite well in the silver fields; that is, until the lode played out. Mary must have either retired rich or gone belly-up like the rest of the town.

The only other building left on the block was Trent's Boardinghouse. However, it looked far too dilapidated to me to venture inside, and I decided to pass.

Having covered every accessible building on the main street of Silver Butte, I considered my work better than half done. I could not complete the job before dark, and I had no intention of rummaging around deteriorating buildings with a flashlight. Therefore, I decided to call a halt to my day's work and finish off the other street the following morning. With a little luck, I could complete my exploration and return to the city before nightfall. Besides, I wanted to take a closer look at a few other spots while I still had good light. There was a nice-looking stream just west of town. I thought I would stroll down and wash off some of the dust I had picked up.

I passed the lodging house and picked my way between a deposit of fist-sized rocks and a pile of old tin cans. There were also some rotted timbers banked up against a small boulder. A short distance beyond stretched a beautiful natural spring with the clearest water I had ever seen. There was a gentle flow to it, and I watched the stream for several minutes as it tumbled over smooth pebbles and a sheet of fine, light brown silt. It originated somewhere far to the north—in the mountains, I assumed—and disappeared into a ravine a few hundred yards to the south.

I removed my cap and struck it against my thigh, shaking the cobwebs from it. Then I brushed off my shirt and pants with my hands, creating small clouds of dust. I rolled up my sleeves and bent down to dip my hands into the water. Despite the heat of the desert, the water was cool to the touch. I did not realize just how hot and sweaty I was until I threw handfuls of water against my face and the back of my neck. It was refreshing, and I felt like lingering there. I removed my handkerchief and dried myself, all the while wondering which was actually the more valuable commodity—water or silver. I concluded that it all depended on an individual's needs at any given time.

Just as I was ready to return to town, I spotted something about ten feet away. There, in the sand, a few inches from the streambed, was a footprint. Surprised, I moved closer. I spotted a second and a third before they disappeared in the soft sand and rocks. I knelt beside one of the prints and examined it, pushing my fingertips against it. It was the distinct impression of a boot, worn at the outer sole and at the rear of the heel. I was no Daniel Boone, but I guessed that it had been made within the last twenty-four hours. I stood up and looked around. There was no sign of life at all in any direction.

I crossed back over the main street and hiked up the slight incline that led to the mine shaft at the foot of the butte. When I got to within a hundred feet of it, I noticed that there was a second shaft farther to the north. Like the main shaft, it, too, was boarded up. A rail started a slight distance from the entrance and disappeared into the darkness of the shaft. An ore cart lay on its side just off to the right of the shaft. Piles of debris lay scattered about, along with rusty lanterns, some worn hand tools, and wooden beams. I picked my way through the rubble until I stood right in front of the entrance. Peering through the cracks in the boards, I could see some fifteen to twenty feet inside. A splintered beam leaned against one wall of the shaft, and a lantern hung from another support. I traced the rails as far as I could until they disappeared into the murky interior. There was enough of a gap for me to squeeze through the boards, but I had no desire to enter the mine, much less explore it.

The stability of its shoring against the tons of mountain above it did not inspire any confidence in me. Satisfied that the mining aspects of Silver Butte could not lend anything of value to Armitage's research, I retreated to the jeep.

I judged that I had close to two hours of light left. I thought that I would set up the grill and have dinner. After that, I could decide where to bed down for the night. Twenty minutes later, I had a pot of coffee going, a can of beans in a pan, and a sirloin on the grill. I had found a level spot in front of the freight office and decided to make the boardwalk my seat during my meal.

A red-tailed hawk suddenly darted past me. I watched it soar just above the rooftop of the restaurant across the street and then dip into a ravine off in the distance. A minute later, I heard a shuffling sound from somewhere off to my left. Glancing up, I was surprised to see a man sauntering up the street leading a burro.

"Howdy," he said with a friendly grin. "I saw your jeep from a way off. Thought I might share your company."

"Hello," I returned.

He moved slowly, as though his feet were bothering him. Carefully, he secured the burro's rope around the nearest hitching post. I noticed that it toted a sizeable pack along with a rifle in a scabbard.

"Name's Juniper," he said, extending his hand.

"John Hazard."

His hand was rough, calloused, but his grip was firm.

He was short, not more than five-foot-six. His face was creased and brown like rawhide. A scraggly gray beard covered his chin and made him appear older than he probably was. I guessed his age at about seventy. He wore a faded white Stetson that was battered and sweat-stained around the crown. He had on a checked shirt, dusty denims, and old boots.

"Coffee smells good," he said, sniffing the air. "I can always tell the caliber of a man by the coffee he makes."

"Sit down. Steak for dinner. You're welcome to join me."

"Steak," he mused as he rubbed his chin. "Haven't had steak for better than two months now."

"I'll just get another plate and cup and take another sirloin from the cooler."

"Wouldn't want to put you out."

"It's no trouble. I welcome the company."

He went through two cups of coffee before I had the steaks ready, and he seemed to enjoy the meal with deep contentment. I watched him as he poked his fork into the last piece of his steak and swirled it around his plate to soak up the juice from the baked beans. I could tell when a man took pleasure in a meal, and I could not recall when I'd seen anyone enjoy one more. As he set his plate on the boardwalk beside him, he nodded in satisfaction.

I offered him more coffee, but he turned his cup over.

"Best meal I ever had. No better fare than steak and beans . . . unless it's ham and eggs."

"Glad you liked it."

"I'm truly obliged," he said with sincerity.

We had spoken very little during the meal, as we were both intent on satisfying our hunger. I was curious, however, about him. "What are you doing out here in the middle of nowhere?"

He jerked a thumb over his shoulder. "Got a shack a couple of miles over the ridge. I've spent the last thirty years in one part or another of this desert."

"Prospector?"

"Used to be, but there's not much left hereabouts. I collect rocks and bottles and sell 'em to a dealer in Barstow."

"You can make a living doing that?"

"Son, I can live off the land if I have to."

I nodded.

"What exactly is it that you're doin' out here? This ain't exactly Palm Springs."

"No, it isn't." I chuckled. "Actually, I'm doing some historical research."

"Out here?" He glanced around him and shrugged. "There's not much left of Silver Butte. It's been picked to the bone—cleaner than a buzzard's roadkill."

"Well, I'm basically after documents—anything that can tell me what life was like when Silver Butte was booming."

"There's money in that?"

"Not exactly. I'm doing it for a writer who wants to learn as much as he can about the town."

"I see. Some of those writers are mighty strange fellows."

I grinned.

"Well, you mind yourself when you go traipsin' through these old buildings. Some of 'em aren't safe."

"Yeah, I've noticed."

"You plannin' on beddin' down here for the night?"

"I am."

"The lobby of the hotel is as good a place as any. I've spent a few nights there from time to time. The desert gets cold when the sun goes down. You can keep warm in there."

"Thanks. I think I'll take your advice."

"Glad to be of help."

"I imagine that you know this town pretty well."

"As well as anybody."

"What about the two shafts back there? Have you been inside?"

"There are three shafts. The third one you can't see from here. They dug it on the northeast side of the butte. Yeah, I've been inside 'em—long time ago. The area is honeycombed with shafts. There's even one that runs under the town itself. They're too dangerous now. You don't want to go near 'em. The shoring's too dicey."

"I don't intend to."

"Well, it's time for me and Harry to be movin' along," he announced as he rose to his feet.

"Harry . . . your burro?"

"That's right. Harry Truman. I named him after the finest president we ever had."

"You may be right about that."

"Say, you wouldn't happen to have any sugar, would you? Harry loves sugar."

"I think I packed some." I walked over to the jeep and found a box of Domino sugar cubes in the grocery bag. "You can keep it," I said, handing it to Juniper.

"Much obliged," he returned as he poured half a dozen cubes into his hand. He strolled over to the burro and extended his open palm. Harry sniffed at the cubes and then picked them out of his master's hand. "I thank you, and Harry thanks you."

"You don't have much light left. You plan to travel at night?"

"The moon's better than half full. Besides, I can walk this desert blindfolded."

"Okay. Good luck. It was nice meeting you."

"The same to you. And thanks for the grub."

I watched Juniper with interest as he loosed Harry's rope and led him off into the desert. Then I washed the plates and cups and returned everything to the jeep. I picked up my sleeping bag, lantern, and flashlight and headed for the hotel. I turned on the lantern and set it on the reservation desk. It cast a nice, soft glow throughout the lobby. It would not do to wake up in the middle of the night in the dark in a strange place. I might make a wrong turn and break a leg. I unfolded my sleeping bag and removed my .38, which I placed on the floor next to me beside my flashlight. I pulled off my shoes and crawled into my bag, where I stretched out, folding my hands under my head. From my position on the hotel floor, I could see the moon rising through one of the hotel windows. It was, as Juniper said, more than half full. I thought it strange that a city dweller like me rarely took notice of such things; however, one who truly lived off the land might rely more on nature. Somewhere off in the mountains, I heard a coyote howl. The sound was natural and oddly soothing. I closed my eyes and slept like a baby.

On the following morning, the moonbeams that had cast their light on the floor beside me had been replaced by bright rays of sunshine. Also, the heat had returned. Slowly, I sat up and glanced around. The hotel lobby looked the same. It probably had not changed in over a hundred years. I unzipped my sleeping bag and laced up my shoes, after first making certain that nothing had crept into them. I returned my gear to the jeep, grabbed a bar of soap and a hand towel, and decided to wash up in the stream. The sky was a bright azure, with only a few wisps of clouds high overhead. The sun was already working hard, baking the desert floor with the force of a blast furnace. Still, the stream was refreshing as I splashed myself liberally in the gently moving current. A cactus wren stopped by for a drink of water. It peered at me curiously and then went on its way.

I strolled back to the jeep, where I removed the grill

and my cooking utensils. I made coffee and fried some eggs. The breakfast tasted good, and I decided that I was feeling pretty comfortable as I lingered over my third cup. A horned toad scurried across the boardwalk beside me and disappeared through a crack in one of the warped planks. He was already busy, more than likely looking to put food on his table, and I concluded that it was time for me to do the same. I had a job to finish.

I stowed my gear and then set out to explore each remaining building in Silver Butte. I made my way to the west end of the side street, where the sign DOCTOR was painted over the door of the first structure. The door hung loosely on its hinges and squealed loudly as I pushed it open. The doctor who had practiced here had apparently left in a hurry, for he had taken little with him. Left behind were a desk and chair, an examination table, and a medicine cabinet with several empty vials in it. There were no papers about and nothing even to indicate the doctor's name.

The next building was a bakery. Nothing remained here but an old oven that must have been too cumbersome to carry away. A liquor supplier had inhabited the next store. As one might expect, nothing had been left behind but some empty bottles and kegs. The next two structures were completely devoid of anything. Without the benefit of signs, I had no idea at all how they had been employed.

Carter's Boardinghouse proved more profitable. Here,

I located a register of names of apparent boarders and prices charged for their lodging. The names were common enough, but I noted nothing familiar in the lot. Perhaps they might have some significance for Armitage.

A second cafe shared a wall with a harness shop. Both buildings, however, had suffered damage from a fire, and there was nothing I could salvage here.

Another saloon—smaller than the one on the main street—occupied the corner lot on the eastern side of the block. It was basically a carbon copy of the first except that an old oil painting of a dancing girl hung on one wall. I brushed away some of the cobwebs that covered it, searching for the name of the artist, but it was far too faded for me to be able to read. I am no art critic, but it did not look worth saving. Off to one side of the room, a few wooden chairs were stacked against one wall, and a broken faro table was turned on its side. I walked through a back room, also empty, and tried the rear door. It was jammed, but I got it open with a good kick. Outside were only some small falling-down sheds and a crumbled wooden bin. I made a final notation, returned to the main street, and took one last look at the town of Silver Butte. Except for the livery, which was a bit apart from the other structures, I felt confident that the town had yielded everything that it had to offer. I had given Armitage his money's worth.

I secured my notes and the valise in the jeep and made the short walk to the only building I had not yet visited. The livery was a two-story structure with warped boards and faded paint. I removed the crossbar from the front doors and pushed against them until they swung on their rusty hinges, revealing a dark interior. A dry, musty odor struck me as I walked inside. Sunlight penetrated through cracks in the roof and walls, forming bars of light on the dirt floor. A dozen or more stalls ran the length of each side of the building. There were some horseshoes on a wooden bench, and a harness hung from a bracket on a post. A fluttering sound caused me to glance upward, where I spotted an owl flitting from one rafter to another, obviously disturbed by the trespasser in its domain. A ladder with two broken steps led up to a loft. I tested the framework; it was anything but sturdy. I had no interest in trying it. I parted, just as I had entered, leaving the livery's resident in peace.

I returned to the jeep and left Silver Butte.

Chapter Three

I made good time on my return trip. I wondered why it always seemed to take less time coming back from a drive than it did going. The sky started to cloud over, and by the time I was twenty minutes outside of Los Angeles, a light rain began to fall. I turned on my windshield wipers and slowed my speed. I was eager to get out of my sweat-stained clothes and into a shower. Then I would fix a good dinner. On the following morning, I would contact Armitage and arrange a time to present him with my findings.

I was about ten minutes from my apartment when I pulled up to a red light. A newspaper stand on the street corner caught my eye. I was not exactly certain what it was I was looking at, but I had enough confidence in my eyesight to pull around the corner and park the jeep. I jumped out, dropped some quarters into the slot, and removed a paper. I stared blankly at the front page for I had no idea how long, but raindrops were starting to fall on the print and blur it. Quickly, I returned to the cover of the jeep, where I rested the newspaper against the steering wheel. Staring back at me was a photograph of Richard Armitage—only it was not Richard Armitage— and next to it was a photograph of me. The headline read: *NOTED AUTHOR MURDERED, Private Investigator Sought for Questioning.*

I went on to read the article in stunned disbelief. The gist of it was that Armitage had been found shot to death in my office on Saturday. It went on to discuss the author's background with an emphasis on some of his major literary credits. There were a few lines about me, *a respected Los Angeles private investigator, whose current whereabouts are unknown.*

I ran through the article again, still disbelieving what it was I had read. I had no idea what was going on, but of one thing I was certain—the man in the newspaper photograph identified as Richard Armitage was not the man I had met last Friday afternoon in Santa Monica. Even if it was an old photograph, it bore no resemblance whatever to the man introduced to me as Armitage. Something was radically wrong, and I needed to sort it out quickly; however, if I turned myself in, I'd get hopelessly entangled in the legal bureaucracy and lose precious time. I had nothing but respect for the LAPD, but, unlike me, they had to do everything by the book, and that took time. Operating as an independent agent, I might well get results—and clear my name—faster.

More than likely, there was a police dragnet out for me, so I could not go to my apartment, and I could not return to my office. It was Sunday afternoon. Leigh was still out of town with her mother, unless she was on her way back to Los Angeles. Pete Cornell, my good friend in the LAPD, would be home with his family. I needed facts. I could only hope that Pete would honor our friendship, even though his first loyalty was to the force.

I drove the jeep another block until I spotted a pay phone. I could leave the area quickly, before anyone traced the call, and it was a safer bet than using my cell, which would act as an instant GPS. I pulled over and parked, glancing around carefully before getting out. Because it was Sunday afternoon and it was raining, the streets were not that crowded. I pulled the brim of my cap a little lower and made my way to the phone, where I punched in Pete's number.

After several rings, Pete's wife, Evelyn, answered. I identified myself and asked to speak to Pete. Evelyn's voice tensed on the other end of the line, but she asked if I was all right. I told her that I was, and I heard her put the phone down. Thirty seconds later, Pete's voice rang over the receiver. "John, where the devil have you been?"

"I've been out of town, Pete. I just saw the paper, and I don't really know anything about any of this."

"You'll have to come in."

"First, I need some answers."

"First, you come in. *Then* you get all the answers you want . . . after I ask *my* questions."

"No dice. I can't clear myself of this mess if I'm sitting in a holding cell. You, of all people, know the drill."

"Hazard, where are you?" His voice had turned shrill.

"I'm talking to you from a pay phone in downtown LA," I told him. "But it won't do you any good to try to locate me, because I don't intend to be found—not while I'm running down a blind alley."

There was a long pause at the other end of the line.

"Talk to me, Pete. Tell me something. Give me a lead."

"You want facts? You got 'em. Richard Armitage was found dead in your office. His body was discovered by the cleaning lady. He was shot twice through the heart with a gun registered to you. And, by the way, your prints are all over it. The coroner puts the time of death at somewhere between one and two on Saturday afternoon. No one has seen you since Friday. You've been in absentia ever since. There's an APB out for you, buddy. Now, do we have reason to talk, or don't we?"

I did not respond. It took a while to digest his words.

"Hazard!"

"Do you think I would kill someone in my own office with my own gun and leave the gun behind with my prints on it?"

"It doesn't matter what *I* think. The DA and the chief are fuming. They want you here—yesterday."

I stood there, a bit numbed by everything he'd told me. He said something else, but all I heard were the raindrops falling on the bill of my cap.

"Hazard!" He almost shouted into the receiver. "Well, what do you have to say for yourself?"

"I'm innocent," I replied, and I hung up the receiver.

The rain seemed to increase as I walked back to the jeep. I could feel its dampness on my shirt and the back of my neck. I removed my cap and ran a hand through my hair. There was only one place for me to go.

Our firm maintained a safe house that we made use of when we wanted to keep a client on ice. We also used it as a courtesy stop for clients from out of town. It was a small bungalow on an all but deserted cul-de-sac in Newport Beach. Charlie Doyle's brother had left it to him, and Charlie had donated it to our firm. There would be no way Charlie would ever give up that info to the police; he'd been a PI way too long. The safe house would be a secure location for me to hole up for the time being.

I also felt comfortable about one other thing—the jeep. My friend Jerry Dodge had arranged for my use of it as his own personal transaction. As such, it would not be on record, and they would have no reason even to contact Jerry. The police would not be looking for me to be driving around the city in a jeep. I pulled away from the curb and headed south.

The sky was heavily overcast by the time I reached my turnoff. I had my headlights on full beam, and the windshield wipers were working steadily. Even though the traffic was light, I had the uneasy feeling that everybody in the city was looking for me. I did my best to avoid driving abreast of another vehicle or stopping too long at intersections. Once a police car passed me. I let up on the accelerator and even changed lanes, but my concerns were unwarranted, for the cruiser turned off the highway and headed down a side street. I released my breath and drove on.

I was still about a mile from the bungalow when I found myself suddenly stuck in traffic—I mean unmoving, gridlock stuck. For several minutes I did not budge an inch. It took another five minutes to cover the next block. I thought that there must be an accident up ahead. After a time, I spotted an old gent wearing a floral-print shirt and some goofy-looking Bermuda shorts walking along the sidewalk in my direction. I rolled down my window and asked if he knew what the delay might be.

"I don't know, Mac," he said with a shrug.

Another five minutes . . . another block.

Cars started to approach in dribs and drabs from the opposite direction. I waved at one of them, and the driver stopped.

"What's the delay up ahead?"

"They're checking cars for someone."

"The police?"

"That's right," he replied before driving on.

I was shaken. How could they know where I was? My office and my apartment were nowhere near here. They could not possibly be looking for me in Newport Beach. After a moment, my panic eased, and I reasoned out the situation. I was becoming paranoid. It had to be someone else the police were after. I settled down and turned on the jeep's radio. Several minutes later, there was a news flash about an attempted bank robbery. The authorities were on the lookout for three men who had tried to tunnel into a bank vault. I turned off the radio and felt some relief, but not for long. Any such search could still result in an identity check, and Pete had said there was an APB out on me. I could ill afford to flash my driver's license. A sharp officer might even spot me simply from my description. I could not go through the checkpoint. For the time being, the bungalow was out of the question.

The first chance I got, I turned down a side street and headed in another direction. I would have to find a place to lie low for a few hours—at least until the police had left the area. A motel was out of the question, and a restaurant or a diner could prove too risky.

I drove aimlessly for a few minutes before remembering an old college buddy of mine, Kit Parsons. Some of the guys in the dorm had nicknamed him Kit Carson, and the handle stuck. We had kept in touch on and off over the years, although I had not seen him for at least six months. Knowing that, if need be, I could rely on his discretion, I spun the steering wheel and made a beeline in his direction.

I might not even need Kit's discretion; he scarcely paid attention to the news or any current events. Kit was odd in the sense that he lived in a kind of time warp. He had little use for modern technology. He had no computer, no cell phone . . . I don't think he'd ever even owned a car. He seemed to be immersed in the fifties/sixties—one of those people who felt more comfortable in the past than in the present. A trivia expert, Kit used to amaze the college crowd with his endless knowledge of old movies and television series. He was, at one time, a fine athlete—he'd loved baseball. In fact, he'd made it to the Triple A level, but a knee injury ended any chance he had of going further. Ever since school, he made his living as a hack writer. He always wanted to do Hollywood screenplays, but he never quite made it. He did get one novel published several years ago. It was far from a raging success, but he never gave up. He managed to survive by selling an occasional short story or crossword puzzle. He lived on a barely seaworthy cabin cruiser down at the marina. It had been left to him by one of his uncles, as I recalled.

Fifteen minutes later, the marina came into view. It had been raining intermittently ever since I left the pay phone, and now it started to drizzle again. The overcast skies created a misty pall over the ocean and made the marina less inviting than usual. Lights were on here and there, their soft auras reflecting off the water in the harbor. Off in the distance, I could see a few sailboats weaving their way around the buoys. A large white yacht knifed cleanly through the blue waves, leaving behind a perfect, plumelike wake.

I parked the jeep in a lot about two hundred yards from the spot where Kit berthed his craft. The area was nearly empty—a few elderly people strolling about, a kid on a bike, and a uniformed security guard. I waited until they were all well on their way before leaving the jeep. The cool salt air struck me as I walked down the sidewalk and headed to the dock. I spotted Kit's cruiser immediately. I'd known it would be there. He never took it out to sea; he was not a boater. I approached cautiously, hoping that Kit would be aboard and alone. When I came alongside, I stopped and listened. I thought I detected the clicking sound of typewriter keys. I knocked on the side of his boat. The clicking sound stopped. A moment later, Kit emerged from his cabin and stepped on deck.

"Hazard!" he said in surprise.

"Hello, Kit. Permission to come aboard?"

"Granted."

I climbed onto the cruiser, and we shook hands. He looked exactly the same as he had in college except that he had put on some weight. His blond hair and friendly smile gave him a youthful appearance. His eyes were large and alert, as though he took in everything of importance.

"I heard about you on the radio. You've been in the news before, but nothing like this."

So he *had* heard the news. How would he react? "I am in a spot of trouble," I admitted.

"You'd better come below," he said easily.

Relieved, I followed him into the cabin, where he waved me to a cushioned bench. His quarters were neat but cramped—a dining table with a lazy Susan laden with condiments, a few chairs, a pair of bunks, and some odds and ends. A portable typewriter sat on one small table, and next to it was stacked a pile of typewritten sheets of paper. Still a Luddite. It was reassuring to know that some things never changed.

Kit poured some steaming coffee into a mug and passed it to me.

I took a few swallows and felt better inside.

"So, what's it all about?" he asked as he pulled up a chair and sat down facing me.

I took a deep breath and for the next five minutes presented him with a resume of my troubles, including the reason for my detour to his place. He listened intently, nodding once in a while but never interrupting. I could see the wheels turning in his head.

"The classic frame," he concluded.

"I agree."

He glanced at the clock on the wall. "We'll tune in to the radio at the top of the hour. Maybe by then the police will have those would-be bank robbers in custody."

"Okay."

"In the meantime, why don't you just relax for a while? You'll be safe enough here."

"Suits me."

Kit leaned back in his chair and seemed to reflect for a moment. "Richard Armitage, you say?"

"That's right."

"He was a good writer."

"I thought so. That was the reason I accepted such an unusual case."

"And now you're on the dodge."

I nodded.

"What about that cop you know . . . can't he help?"

"Pete Cornell. No, I already tried talking to him. He's an all-right guy, but he's still a cop and can be hardheaded. He wants me to turn myself in."

"Is that such a bad idea?"

"At the moment, it is. I'm totally in the dark right now. I don't even know the rules of the game. No, I'm going to have to stay on the streets for a while."

"Do you want me to try to get you out of the country until the heat is off? We could head down the coast for Mexico."

"No, Kit. I'm not running anywhere. The answers to my questions lie right here. I plan to stay and clear myself."

He breathed a sigh of relief. "I'm glad to hear it. I don't think the *Emma P* would make it out of the harbor, let alone out of the country."

We both laughed out loud.

Kit picked up a pencil and rolled it over in his fingers. "You say you met Armitage?"

"I met someone who claimed to be Armitage, but the picture of Armitage in the newspaper didn't look anything like the man I met."

"Interestingly enough, I met him myself once."

My eyes widened.

"It was a long time ago—at least twenty-five years— at a bookstore in La Jolla. He was doing a signing. I bought a copy of his book. It was called *California's Lost*

Trails." Kit paused for a moment. "How did he talk?" he asked.

"What do you mean?"

"His conversation."

"He had a nice, deep, sonorous voice. He seemed to be a good conversationalist. Why?"

"No speech impediment?"

"No."

"That's interesting, because when I talked to him, he had one of the worst cases of stammering I'd ever heard."

"Stammering?" I echoed.

"Yeah. In fact, I always thought that that was the reason he was so reclusive. A brilliant writer but a poor oral communicator. I don't recall even seeing an author photo on any of his book jackets."

"Now that you mention it, I don't either. Of course, he could have had speech therapy to correct the problem," I suggested.

"He could have, but if he did, why did he continue to dwell in such obscurity? A writer has to do everything he can to promote his publications—lectures, presentations, television, radio . . ."

"Good point. That adds credence to my suspicion that the man I met was not Armitage."

"I'd say so."

I took another sip of coffee as I considered the information Kit had presented. My gaze wandered around the cabin, as did my thoughts. When I finally focused on the typewriter, I asked, "Are you working on another novel?"

"Yeah, actually, I am."

"What's it about?"

"It's a manuscript for a *Man from U.N.C.L.E.* paperback."

"*The Man from U.N.C.L.E.* . . . I remember that show. I always liked it. That went off the air back in the sixties, didn't it?"

"That's right."

"Well, they're not publishing those books anymore, are they?"

"No, they stopped a long time ago."

"Then why are you wasting your time on such a project?"

He shrugged. "Actually, it's a kind of mental exercise. It helps me stay focused on certain aspects of the past and keeps the details fresh in my mind. Besides, there are always remakes of movies and old television series. Who knows? Such a manuscript might just come into demand again."

"It doesn't seem very likely. The Cold War's been over for some time now. Secret agents aren't in demand the way they once were."

"True, but interesting characters and quality stories never go out of style."

"You could be right about that. You still good on your trivia?"

He leaned back in his chair and smiled. "Try me."

"All right. What was the name of the town where Lucas McCain lived in *The Rifleman*?"

"North Fork."

"What was Robert Conrad's name in *Hawaiian Eye*?"

"Tom Lopaka."

"In what series did Mike Connors star before he was on *Mannix*?"

"*Tightrope.*"

"In the 1954 movie *The Garden of Evil,* what was the name of the fishing village where the ship broke down?"

"Puerto Miguel."

"In *Twenty Thousand Leagues Under the Sea,* what was Kirk Douglas' name?"

"Ned Land."

"In *The Magnificent Seven,* what actor played the part of Harry?"

"Brad Dexter."

"What was Humphrey Bogart's last film?"

"*The Harder They Fall.*"

We went on and on for several minutes, but I was unable to stump Kit with any of my questions. Finally, I threw up my hands and congratulated him. We chuckled about the matter, and he said, "You know, Hazard, you've rekindled some of the good old days." He sighed and then added, "I guess I've become a bit of a dinosaur."

"How do you mean?"

"Well, remember how all the guys in the dorm used to drop by and ask me all those TV and movie questions?"

"Yeah. You were the ultimate authority."

He shrugged. "Today, there's no reason to consult someone like me. Pushing a few buttons on a computer keyboard will get you all the information you need about anything . . . and then some."

"That's true, I suppose, but then again, the impression you remembered from meeting Armitage wasn't something I likely could have gotten from a computer. Your memory and your attention to detail support my suspicion, and you've given me something to work on."

He got a wistful look in his eye. "It's the top of the hour. Let's try the radio."

We listened for several minutes. Finally, the newscaster announced that the search for the would-be bank robbers had come to a successful conclusion. They had been apprehended not six blocks from the tunnel they had constructed.

Kit turned off the radio.

"Well, that takes care of your checkpoint problem, anyway."

"Yeah, and I'd best be on my way."

"You're welcome to spend the night if you like. I'm not the best cook, but there's a good Italian restaurant nearby. I could have some pizza or spaghetti and meatballs delivered."

"No thanks. I can't put you on the spot any longer.

Harboring me from the police could get you into plenty of hot water."

I extended my hand, and he took it.

"Maybe the next time we meet will be under more comfortable circumstances," I said. "Thanks again."

"Thank you, John," he returned, a smile on his face.

Chapter Four

I had not been to the safe house for over three months, but everything looked the same as I pulled into the driveway and parked under the carport behind the bungalow. I carried a key on my chain for the dwelling, and I quickly unlocked the back door. I reached inside and flipped on the porch light and an inside light. The porch light cast a nice, soft glow all the way to the jeep.

I stepped into a small kitchen equipped with the usual appliances. It had everything but a microwave. I passed through the kitchen and entered a dining room with a table and chairs for four. It, in turn, opened into a living room with a pair of comfortable armchairs and a sofa. I closed all the drapes before I turned on one of the end-table lamps. Then I did a walk-through of the rest of the house—two small bedrooms and a bath. Everything looked neat and orderly.

I retreated to the jeep for the cooler and the bag of food. I placed the rest of the meat in the refrigerator and unpacked the remaining groceries and left them on the counter. I returned to the jeep for my last clean outfit and my .38. Then I locked the back door, turned off the porch light, and headed directly for the shower.

Fifteen minutes later, I felt human again. I shaved, brushed my teeth, and got dressed. I went into the living room and turned on the television. I found the local station I usually watched for the early-evening news and waded through half a dozen commercials, an abbreviated weather forecast, and an interview with a psychologist about the rehab problems of a teenage actress. Finally, the announcer related the news I had been waiting for. A photograph of Richard Armitage was flashed on the screen—the same one that was printed earlier in today's newspaper. My photograph appeared next. It was about five years old, taken when I had reached a successful conclusion to an extortion case. The newscast added little to what had already appeared in the morning paper except that it provided a bit more background on Armitage's life, listing in particular some of the literary awards he had received. The broadcaster also referred to me as "a highly respected private investigator" and went on to list my age and description. The accolade was pleasant enough, but regardless of one's reputation and credentials, it never looks good when the police are pursuing you for questioning and your whereabouts are unknown.

I turned off the set and leaned back in the armchair, closing my eyes in order to think. It was obvious that someone had wanted me out of town long enough to orchestrate the murder of Armitage and frame me in the process. The problem was that I had no connection whatever with Richard Armitage. We had never before crossed paths. Therefore, there had to be somewhere else to look. There had to be a common denominator, a bridge that linked the two of us.

The footsteps came from the driveway. They were soft, yet I heard them clearly enough. Someone was approaching the bungalow. I remained in the chair, motionless, straining to follow the sound, but it stopped. Then, after about thirty seconds, I heard something again—this time near the back door. I turned off the lamp and edged my way to the kitchen. I had left my .38 on the counter next to the refrigerator. The lights were off in the kitchen, but I felt my way along the countertop until I found the gun. I moved behind the back door and waited. A full minute passed before I heard the knob turn. Metal scraped against metal; there was a click, and the door opened. I waited. Finally, someone stepped into the kitchen. I slipped the .38 under my belt and knelt down. In one rapid sequence, I slammed the door, grabbed a pair of ankles, and pulled hard. There was a grunting sound followed by a dull thud as the silhouetted intruder struck the linoleum. I heard a short intake of breath and then silence. I found the light switch and then looked down at the outstretched figure in surprise.

Quickly, I knelt down beside Leigh and turned her gently. Cradling her head with one hand, I brushed away her hair with the other. She moaned in pain, then opened her eyes and forced a smile. "Hi, boss. Do you always greet your guests in this fashion?" she asked glibly.

"Leigh, I'm sorry. I didn't know. Forgive me if I hurt you."

"I'm all right . . . just had the wind knocked out of me," she said, taking a deep breath.

I picked her up and carried her into the living room, where I set her on the sofa. I turned on the lamp and sat beside her. At the moment, she looked very vulnerable, almost fragile. She was wearing a white blouse, a pair of light blue slacks, and some black pumps. A small bump was starting to form on her forehead, just about where her blond bangs ended. I retreated to the kitchen, found a dish towel, and doused it with cold water. In a moment, I had it pressed against Leigh's forehead while I repudiated myself for my rashness.

"How did you know I was here?"

"I figured it was the only place you could go." She looked at me with slightly upturned lips. "I haven't been the secretary to LA's top private eye for five years for nothing, you know."

I smiled at her. "Private *investigator*," I corrected her. She grinned.

"Good girl," I said, patting her arm.

"John, I heard all about you on television and on the radio. What happened? What's going on?"

I shrugged. "I wish I knew, but right about now, it

looks as though I'm shaping up to be the patsy of the year."

She frowned, deep concern in her large brown eyes.

Briefly, I recapped everything that had happened since the last time I talked to her.

She digested every word carefully, interrupting a few times to ask questions. Finally, she said, "You've been had, all right. The question is . . . how are you going to clear yourself?"

"Well, it won't be easy, since I'm on the lam. I'll have to rely on you to do some of my legwork."

"You always have."

"Yeah, but this time things are different. We'll be working in a fishbowl. The police will be watching the office, my apartment, maybe even your place."

"We've been in tight spots before."

"We have, sure enough, but I've got a feeling that this one is going to put a real squeeze on us."

She reached out and placed a hand on my arm. "I'm glad you said 'us.' "

"I have my doubts about involving you. Pete Cornell is steamed enough to make things tough on you if he knows you're even in contact with me."

"That's not like him."

"He's got a job to do. He wouldn't be a good cop if he didn't go by the book."

"But you're friends. The two of you go way back."

"We'll still be friends when this is over, no matter

what, but Pete can't let his personal feelings for me override his professional responsibility."

She nodded. "All right. What's our first move?"

"Richard Armitage. We find out who wanted him out of the way. Who, in particular, would benefit from his death?"

"I'll get right on it. What will you be doing in the meantime?"

"I'm going back to Santa Monica tonight—to the house where I met the man who *claimed* to be Richard Armitage." I located the business card with the phone number that the alleged Darrin Thomas had given me to contact Armitage, and I scribbled the address I'd visited on the back. "Find out who really lives at this address. I'm guessing the telephone number might match the address."

"Why not send the police to the house?"

"For one thing, I have no proof of anything yet, and right now my credibility doesn't look too impressive. For another, I doubt that the two men I met are anywhere within miles of that location."

"Then why go there at all?"

"In case they left some clue behind that might put me on to them. It's a long shot, but it's worth a try. Right now, I've got nothing else to go on."

"I guess you're right, but I don't like the idea." She passed her hand over her forehead and flinched as she felt the bruise.

"You'll have a nice little bump there for a while."

"Maybe it will add character to my face," she said, forcing a smile.

"Thanks for offering to help. You know, this goes beyond the typical employer-employee relationship."

"We're a team, remember? Now, how about if I fix us something to eat?"

"You needn't bother. I can cook for myself."

"Actually, I do need to bother. I've been so worried, I haven't eaten since breakfast."

"Well, in that case . . ."

"What have you got?"

"I have a big steak left and some lunch meat. There's bread and coffee too."

"That'll do just fine. I'm hungry enough to eat leather."

"I'll fix the coffee."

"I'll start the steak and make some sandwiches too."

In no time we were comfortably seated at the dining room table with a nice little spread in front of us. Leigh had done a good job on the steak, which we split. It proved to be both tender and tasty. We chatted casually over the meal—about her mother, San Luis Obispo, even the weather—any number of topics just to get our minds off the problem at hand. I had to admit, I managed to relax a bit, and I enjoyed her company. She was the best secretary I'd ever had, and she was more, much more. The two of us approached problems from different angles. She was more analytical, relying on the computer and her data systems. I was more of an old-fashioned, seat-of-the-pants type of investigator. Whereas Leigh preferred to study an individual from a paper printout, I relied more on the expression on his face or the tone of his voice. There were times when we were both right; there were times when we were both wrong. I guess it all just came down to a matter of style.

Leigh offered to wash the dishes, but I urged her toward the door, reminding her that she had work to do.

"Remember," I cautioned, "when you call—"

"I know. Use a pay phone, not the office phone, and not my cell. No need to advertise my movements to anyone who might be keeping track."

"Exactly. And the next time you come here . . ."

"Don't worry, boss. I know how to lose a tail."

I smiled at her admiringly.

She smiled back, but beneath those nicely upturned lips lay a subtle fear that caused a slight twitch in her face. Her eyes were moist with concern as she pressed her fingers into my arm. I wanted to tell her to get into her car and drive back to San Luis Obispo until this whole thing blew over, but I knew she would never do such a thing—not while I was on the spot. That was the kind of person she was. I walked her to her car and watched until her taillights disappeared into the darkness.

The rain had stopped, and the night sky had all but cleared; only a few scudding clouds lingered in what was shaping up to be another beautiful southern California night. A pale yellow aura surrounded the moon, and stars were beginning to reveal themselves. The sky made me feel hopeful as I rolled down the window of the jeep and headed back to Santa Monica. I did not know if my return to the house where I had encountered the man who called himself Richard Armitage would prove fruitful or turn out to be a wild goose chase. My guess was the latter, but there was nothing better I had to do this evening. Besides, I had no intention of hiding myself away in the bungalow, staring at the patterns on the wallpaper.

The house was in darkness when I drove by, as I'd expected it would be. I circled the block a few times to get a better feel for the neighborhood. Finally, I parked a block away and walked down the sidewalk on the opposite side of the street, avoiding one particularly bright lamppost, before I crossed over and strolled up the driveway. I made my way to the back door of the house. A wooden fence around the rear of the property afforded me the privacy I needed, and I felt comfortable about using my flashlight without fear of being seen by any curious neighbor. The door was secured with a standard lock. With the array of picks I'd brought, I figured to have it open within a few minutes, and I set to work. It actually took me seven minutes, but I ultimately did gain entry and quickly shut the door behind me. I stood in the darkness for a long moment, listening, as I guided the beam of the flashlight around the room. Silence surrounded me. I was in a kitchen. It all looked very bare—no small appliances or cookware on the countertops. Soundlessly, I crossed the room and entered a dining area, where I found the furniture draped in sheets. I went from room to room, encountering exactly the same scenario everywhere in the house. Everything was empty of life, as though no one had been here for months. Eventually, my search took me to the library, where I had had my first meeting with the man I'd thought was Richard Armitage and his so-called secretary, Darrin Thomas. Here, too, the furniture was covered. Even the bookcases, which I had admired so much, were draped. I found it all very frustrating. I pulled the sheets off the desk and one of the tables and opened every drawer, sifting through the contents, yet I came across nothing more than standard stationery, a calendar, and some pens and pencils. There was nothing of a personal nature to identify the house's owner. I considered that there might be a wall safe somewhere containing important documents, but I was not skilled enough to crack it; therefore, I did not even bother to pursue such an angle. In the movies and on television, a private investigator always seems to discover a clue that leads to a solution for the case—a matchbook with the name of a nightclub printed on it, old mail or a receipt for a purchase. I had no such luck.

I left the library and crossed back into the hallway, which led me to the foyer. It was here that I noticed something I had missed when I first passed through. There were black scuff marks on the tile. I directed the beam of my flashlight over them and followed their trail. It ended abruptly at the door of what I assumed was a closet. I opened it and shined the flashlight inside.

Startled, I took a step backward and grunted loudly. Crammed inside was the body of a man. His arms and legs were twisted bizarrely at his sides, his head and one of his shoulders pressed awkwardly against one wall. There was a large wound on his forehead, and a considerable amount of blood had congealed as it had drained over his face and onto his shirt. He appeared to be about sixty, but his contorted face distorted his features, making it difficult to be certain. I moved closer and knelt down. I felt his skin. It was cold to the touch. I went through his pockets until I found a wallet. In it were credit cards and two twenty-dollar bills. His driver's license listed his name as Henry Waller. His age was sixty-two, and his address was in Culver City. I committed it to memory, wiped the wallet and its contents with my handkerchief, and then returned it to where I had found it.

I left the house the same way I had entered, wiping clean everything I might have touched. I walked back to the jeep and drove away.

I found the nearest pay phone and placed a call to the homicide division. I reported my find to the sergeant who took my call. When he asked for my name, I hung up.

Chapter Five

At eleven o'clock the following morning, Leigh called.

"I'm at a public phone about a mile away. Is it okay if I come over now?"

"Yes, I'm waiting. Were you followed?"

"I was. An unmarked green Chevy. I lost it on the freeway."

"Good. See you soon."

Five minutes later, I met her at the back door.

"I thought you could use some extra odds and ends," she said as she handed me a large bag of groceries, which I accepted and placed on the counter.

"I appreciate it."

She looked rested and refreshed as she flashed a nice smile at me. A slight bruise on her forehead was the only noticeable reminder of her mishap from the previous evening. She wore a light blue blouse decorated with a dark blue outline of a swan stitched just over her heart. A matching skirt that fell a couple of inches above her knees made her look respectably appealing.

"The phone's been ringing off the hook—reporters. They all want a story. One of them even showed up at the office with a camera crew. I told them that I didn't know where you were or anything at all about the matter. I informed them that I had just returned from an out-of-town trip and knew only what I had heard in the media."

"That's about all you can do for the time being."

We sat down at the dining room table over coffee as she briefed me on her findings.

"Richard Armitage was a well known and extremely successful writer. He was held in high regard in literary circles, although he was a bit of a recluse. As far as I could find, there were only a few existing photos of him. The one in the newspaper you already saw, and this is the other," she said, removing a printout from her purse and pushing it across to me.

I studied it carefully. "This is not the man I met last Friday."

She nodded. "Armitage was sixty-five."

"The man I met looked closer to eighty."

"An imposter."

"Yeah. What else did you learn about him?"

"He traveled a lot—mostly throughout California and Nevada. He was thorough in researching his work, and he was known for his meticulous attention to details."

"I can bear testimony to that. I respected and enjoyed his books."

"He was married. His wife died ten years ago. There were no children. He had two nephews—Myron and Joe Bendix—his only living relatives."

"Never heard of them."

"Myron is clean. He's thirty-eight, owns a small florist shop in downtown Los Angeles. He's divorced and has two children. His ex moved back East and took the youngsters with her. Joe, on the other hand, did time for forging his uncle's name on some checks. I had Warden Raines fax his mug shot to me." She pulled the fax from her purse and laid it in front of me.

"You've been busy," I said, smiling at her.

"I try to earn my salary. Speaking of which, I could do with a raise."

"We'll discuss it later—if I still have any control over my finances when the dust settles."

"I'll take that as a maybe."

"Tom Raines is a good man," I said as I turned the photo around and studied it closely.

"I know the two of you go back a long way."

"This looks like the man who introduced himself to me as Darrin Thomas, Armitage's secretary. The hair and the mustache match, and he was wearing wire-rimmed glasses like the ones in this mug shot. But I can't be a hundred percent certain. The lighting wasn't the best when I saw him."

"Joe Bendix is forty. He has an IQ of one sixty-eight," she continued. "He never held a job for more than two years and seems to be a bit of a freeloader."

"Still, I see no connection."

"Well, there is one. Lucky for you, about three years ago, I cross-referenced all of your old files and fed them into a computer program that I designed. Bendix was in the same cell block with someone you had sent up—a Manny Gorzik."

I could not help but let out a low whistle. "Manny Gorzik . . . but he's still behind bars."

"Not anymore. I checked back with Warden Raines. Gorzik was released three months ago—for good behavior."

"Good behavior! Manny?"

She nodded. "That's not all. The warden confirmed that Bendix and Gorzik got pretty chummy."

"Brains and brawn—a lethal combination."

"Gorzik was before my time. I read about his case in your files. You helped send him up for an attempted armored-car robbery."

"That's right. Manny was a would-be pro wrestler. His moniker was 'The Quake.' He weighs two hundred seventy pounds and has the arms of a gorilla."

"He weighs two-eighty now."

I eyed her in surprise.

"The warden said that Gorzik was the only inmate who liked prison food."

"It figures."

" 'The Quake' . . . sounds formidable."

I grinned.

"What's so amusing?"

"There's an inside joke about Manny that only a small circle knows. He wasn't called 'The Quake' because the ground shook beneath him when he walked or because of the way he body-slammed his opponents. Manny acquired his nickname because of a phobia."

"A phobia?"

"Yes. You see, Manny has a deep-seated fear of earthquakes. Even the slightest tremor is enough to send him over the edge. He breaks out in a sweat, starts to hyperventilate . . . he's just reduced to a bowl of mush. The image is a bit incongruous—a big hulking bruiser of a man having a meltdown because of the shifting of some subterranean plates."

"What kind of character with such a fear of earthquakes decides to live in California?" Leigh asked.

I shook my head. "Maybe he had nowhere else to go."

"At his trial, he threatened to kill you—or so the file said."

"He wasn't the first."

"He blamed you for his arrest?"

"That, along with the fact that he took a slug in the kneecap during the heist. It ended any possible career he might have had in the ring."

"That's too bad, but . . ." She looked at me questioningly.

"It was my bullet that shattered his kneecap," I said by way of explanation.

"Oh, I see."

"Anything else?"

"Yes. Lieutenant Cornell dropped by the office. He asked me a zillion questions, then gave me a brief lecture about aiding a fugitive from justice. But finally he mellowed a bit and spoke to me off the record. He's really worried about you, boss. He's afraid some police officer might get overanxious and shoot you."

I nodded.

"Do you think I should turn over this information to him? After all, he does have your best interests at heart."

"He's probably already aware of it."

"Why? What do you mean?"

I took a swallow of coffee and then pushed my cup aside. "Pete Cornell knows I didn't kill Richard Armitage. He'll reason everything out the same way that we did. First, he'll look for those who would benefit from Armitage's death. Then he'll check out anybody who has a grudge against me. That will tie Joe Bendix to Manny Gorzik. Believe me, he's doing the legwork right now."

"In that case, all you have to do is sit tight."

"I've never been very good at that. Besides, two heads are better than one. I might be able to turn up something on my own."

"I don't like it."

"Trust me when I tell you that I don't either. It isn't easy being your own client, especially when the entire Los Angeles police force is looking for you."

She wrapped her fingers around her cup tightly but then relaxed her grip. "By the way, Alice Doyle also called this morning. She's quite worried about you. I did my best to put her mind at ease."

"Good. I don't want Charlie involved in this. He's sixty-seven, and he struggles with rheumatoid arthritis."

"Charlie doesn't know anything about it. He's on a fishing trip in the Sierras with his grandsons. Alice doesn't expect him back for a few days yet."

"It's just as well."

"Maybe you should bring in some help. I'm sure Syd Carruthers would be glad to lend a hand."

"If things reach that stage, I will, but not just yet. I don't want Syd to risk having his license suspended because of me. He's got a wife and four kids to support."

"Yeah, well, sooner or later, you're going to have to stop worrying about your friends and start worrying about yourself."

"When the time comes."

She shrugged. "Anything you say, but I think I should call Lieutenant Cornell this afternoon. Maybe we can pool some of our information."

"I guess it can't hurt to try . . . providing that he's in a forgiving mood. By the way, did you find out who lives at that address in Santa Monica?"

"Yes," she said, almost as an afterthought. "The owner of the residence is named Martinson."

"It doesn't ring any bells. See if you can establish a connection between the owner and Manny Gorzik—or this Joe Bendix, Armitage's nephew, who did time with Gorzik."

"Right."

"And here's another name for you," I said, handing her a piece of paper.

"Henry Waller . . . who's he?"

"I don't know, but I found his body last night at the house in Santa Monica."

"What!"

"It looked as though he had been bludgeoned to death. I phoned it in to the police—anonymously."

She shook her head. "The bodies are starting to pile up."

"Yeah."

She sipped her coffee and stared off at something across the room as though lost in thought.

"Don't worry too much, Leigh. At least, we seem to be making progress."

She nodded halfheartedly. "What's your next move?

I considered the question. "I'm gambling that Pete Cornell already has Manny Gorzik and Joe Bendix under surveillance. I won't have much chance of getting anywhere near them. It's less likely, however, that Pete is interested in Myron Bendix, Armitage's clean-living nephew. I think I'll drop in on him. He just might be able to furnish me with some helpful information. Got a listing for his shop?"

"Yes. It's called The Corner Florist." She gave me the address.

"All right. I'll pay him a visit. Let's say we meet again tomorrow at this same time to compare notes."

She nodded.

"Oh, and one more detail. Check back with Tom Raines. Ask him if Joe Bendix walks with a limp."

"Right. Anything else?"

"Not for the time being."

She reached for her cup, took another swallow, and then stood up. "Until tomorrow, then."

I put on my Dodgers cap and sunglasses and headed for downtown LA. I knew the neighborhood of Myron Bendix's shop well, but I was not familiar with The Corner Florist itself. An empty parking space under the outstretched branches of a shade tree afforded me a location that was close by and reasonably secluded. I moved cautiously down the block, pausing on occasion to glance into storefront windows, using the reflections in the glass panes to check my back for signs of any of Pete Cornell's plainclothesmen, but I saw no one. I knew most of his boys, plus a good number of other detectives on the force, and I figured I had a fifty-fifty chance of spotting one of them before I was noticed. The odds were reasonable, and I had to play them.

Eventually, I found myself standing in front of The Corner Florist, a small shop with a handsome display of vividly colored flowers in the showcase. An elderly woman emerged with a basket spilling over with daisies, and a moment later, a teenage boy passed through the door carrying a corsage in a plastic container. As far as I could tell, the shop was empty save for one man who walked past the window with a planter, which he placed on one of the shelves. I assumed he was Myron Bendix. He was of average build and completely bald. According to Leigh's information, he was thirty-eight, but he appeared to be much older—perhaps because of his lack of hair. He wore a white shirt with a black bow tie and seemed intent on adjusting his floral arrangements. I meandered in, glanced around, and then approached the counter.

"May I be of any help?" the man asked, greeting me with a smile.

"Are you Myron Bendix?" I asked.

"Yes, what can I do for you?"

I stared at him carefully through my sunglasses. There was more than a passing resemblance between him and his brother.

"I'd like to buy a dozen long-stemmed roses."

"Of course." He strolled over to one of the showcases and suggested a particular variety, making some esoteric remarks that I did not understand.

"Those will do fine," I replied.

"Splendid. Will you be taking them with you?"

"No, I'd like them delivered."

He stepped behind the counter, where he pulled out an order form. "Now, what is the name and address?"

"Leigh Masters," I said, and I provided him with my office address.

I watched him as he jotted down the information.

"Will you be paying with cash or credit?"

"Cash."

He gave me the price, and I paid him.

"The flowers will arrive this afternoon," he announced as he produced my change. "Will there be any message?"

"No, just sign it John."

"Very good."

"Mr. Bendix?"

"Yes?" he replied, eyeing me closely.

"My name is Hazard."

Suddenly, his face twitched, and he took half a step backward.

"I wanted to ask you some questions about your brother."

"I thought there was something familiar about you. Your picture was in the paper. You're a wanted man. You killed my uncle!"

"I didn't kill your uncle."

"You'd better leave! I don't have to answer any of your questions."

"No, you don't, but I happen to be an innocent man, and I believe that your brother had something to do with the trouble I'm in."

"I don't believe that."

"I never met your uncle. I had no reason to kill him. Your brother, on the other hand, would stand to inherit half of his estate."

"As would I, but that doesn't make me a murderer."

"Your brother's already taken advantage of your uncle. He's done time because of it. There must have been hard feelings between them."

"That doesn't make him a murderer."

"No, but it shows that he had motive."

"I don't know anything about that," he said, moving toward his telephone. "If you don't leave, I'll be forced to call the police. They've already been here, you know."

"I'm sure they have. All right, I'll leave, but before I do, I'd like you to answer one question. Do you believe that your brother is capable of killing your uncle?"

"No . . . I mean . . . I don't know. Joe and I never got on very well. We don't have much to do with each other."

"Did you visit him while he was in prison?"

"Yes, of course I did. After all, he's still my brother."

"Did he ever mention another inmate named Manny Gorzik?"

"Manny . . . no . . . I don't know . . . he might have," he answered nervously. "The police asked me that same question. I don't remember."

"I believe that your brother and Manny Gorzik framed me for your uncle's murder."

"I . . . I don't know what to think. I shouldn't be talking to you. I'm phoning the police."

I stood there for a moment as he picked up the receiver. I concluded that there was nothing more I could learn from him, and I left.

I had been back at the bungalow for a little over an hour when I heard a tapping at the back door. I knew it could not be Leigh. She would never alter our arrangements without alerting me first, and no one else knew where I was. I picked up my .38 and passed through the kitchen. When I parted the curtains on the window, I was relieved and surprised to see Lou Kaiser standing there. Quickly, I unlocked the door and admitted him.

"Hiya, Hazard," he said with a smile as he sidled inside carrying what looked like some dry cleaning encased in plastic slung over his shoulder and a shoe box under his arm.

"What are you doing here, Lou?"

"Things were getting a little hot for Leigh. Cornell's boys are sticking to her like glue. She dropped by the diner to talk things over with Barney. She said you could use some fresh threads, but she didn't dare go anywhere near your apartment and then come to see you. Instead, she called your tailor. He picked out some items in your size from his stock. Barney told me to take his car and pick 'em up for you."

"Thanks. That was good thinking on Leigh's part."

"It's just a sports coat, some pants, and a couple of dress shirts and ties. Your tailor even pressed 'em for you."

"Great."

"Oh, and there's a pair of loafers in here," he said, holding out the box. "Where should I put everything?"

I pointed to the hallway closet.

"You want to stay for lunch?"

He grinned. "I haven't had breakfast yet."

"Sit down. Leigh brought me groceries. I'll throw something together."

"Oh, I almost forgot. Barney sent you some chili. I left it in the car."

"Well, you can't have chili for breakfast. Bring it in and put it in the refrigerator. I'll eat it later. How about some ham and eggs for now?"

"Sounds good."

Fifteen minutes later, we sat down to a hearty meal of coffee, toast, fried eggs, and Virginia baked ham. Lou ate hungrily and drank four cups of coffee. He loved coffee and seemed to drink gallons of it every day. I never knew where he put all the food he ate. Finally, after both of us slowed down, we talked a little about my situation.

"Leigh seems worried, Hazard. How are you going to get out of this?"

"I don't know, Lou. I think I'm starting to figure out some of the angles, but knowing what happened and proving it are two different things—especially when I can't even walk the streets without looking over my shoulder."

"I'll be glad to do whatever I can—you know that."

"I appreciate it, but enough people are already sticking their necks out for me."

"You've done plenty for me over the years. That's why I'm here."

"Thanks, Lou."

"Oh, by the way, I have a message for you. Leigh said that I should tell you that Joe Bendix walks with a limp, that he injured his leg in a car accident ten years ago. Is that what you wanted to know?"

I nodded.

"Does that help you?"

"It might."

"Who's Joe Bendix?"

"It looks like he's the one who masterminded this frame."

"He got some kind of grudge against you?"

"None at all. In fact, I've never met him. It appears to be a crime of mutual convenience."

He pushed his cup away and leaned back in his chair. "How's that?"

"Joe Bendix seems to have gone into partnership with an old acquaintance of mine—Manny Gorzik."

"Gorzik! That gorilla?"

"That's right."

"Whew! He was a nasty one. I once saw him wrestle. He looked like he could twist a fire hydrant into a knot."

"Yeah."

"You don't want to tangle with him."

"Believe me, I don't. I thought he was still in stir."

"Maybe you'd be better off turning yourself in. A nice, warm cell could look pretty good compared to a face-off with The Quake."

"Now, you're beginning to sound like Leigh."

"Well, you have to admit, there's some merit to the idea."

I nodded.

He stood up and adjusted his belt. "I'd best be goin' now. You can always reach me through Leigh or Barney."

I shook his hand.

"By the way, how did that horse do—Robin's Arrow?"

Lou frowned. "He finished out of the money."

Chapter Six

After Lou left, I cleared the table and washed the dishes. I then went into the living room and sat down in one of the armchairs to think. The drapes were still drawn, and it was dark. I generally thought better in the dark. Two murders. Leigh was right: the bodies were beginning to pile up. Who was Henry Waller, and what exactly did he have to do with the men who'd set me up? Was he part of a scheme that had turned sour, or was he someone who happened to be in the wrong place at the wrong time? After fifteen minutes, I decided that there was no use racking my brain over the matter any longer. There was just not enough for me to go on. I decided to wait and see what Leigh might turn up.

I turned on the television to look for the local news broadcast. Maybe there would be more information on the Armitage murder. I was about ten minutes too early for the broadcast, so I surfed through a couple of channels until I came across an afternoon movie. I recognized it at once as *Jane Eyre* with Joan Fontaine and Orson

Welles. I had always loved Orson Welles' sonorous voice. I watched and listened for several minutes, and then something struck me. Richard Armitage or, at least, the man who had posed as Armitage, had a similar voice—not quite as rich or distinctive, but elegant—a trained voice. I leaned forward and listened more closely to Orson Welles deliver his "Grace Poole's patient" speech. It was then that it came to me. I knew where I had heard that voice before. It was Shakespeare . . . Lear, in fact. I had seen an actor portray King Lear at the Pasadena Playhouse about ten years ago. His name was Tracy . . . Lawrence Tracy. I had only seen him a few times. I doubted that he'd ever made it big, but I was always impressed with his voice.

We kept a telephone directory in a side table. Excitedly, I took it out and paged through it but found no listing for a Lawrence Tracy. I had a friend in the theater business—Rudy Kamfer. Luckily, he was listed, and I dialed his number. There was no answer. I turned the television channel back to the local news. A few minutes into the broadcast, there was a brief mention of the case, but the commentator offered little additional information than that which had appeared on the previous day. I listened to the weather and the sports. Then I dialed again. This time, Rudy answered.

"Rudy, this is John Hazard."

"John! You're hotter than an Academy Award winner. How does it feel?"

"I'm beginning to suffer from the burn."

"What's it all about?"

"Rudy, as soon as I find out, I'll explain it over lunch— once I clear my name, that is."

"Good luck. How can I help?"

"I'm trying to run down a stage actor by the name of Lawrence Tracy."

"Larry Tracy . . . sure, I remember him. Haven't seen him in years. I doubt that he's still in the business."

"Any idea how I can locate him?"

"His one-time agent is a friend of mine—Milt Burroughs. Hold on a sec. I'll give you his private number."

Thirty seconds later, Rudy read me the telephone number of Burroughs, and I thanked him.

"Just tell him I told you to call. Oh, and listen, buddy, if they make a movie about you over this Armitage thing, I want first crack at signing you."

"You've got it, Rudy."

A minute later I had Milt Burroughs on the line. I explained that Rudy had referred me to him, and I avoided giving him my name. He seemed cooperative enough.

"Lawrence Tracy . . . yeah, I used to handle the guy. He had talent, all right, but he didn't want to work to develop it. He didn't want to attend any drama classes, and he missed too many rehearsals. He liked the bottle too much. I lost track of him three or four years back. Couldn't do much for a guy like that, if you know what I mean."

"Yeah, I've heard the story before. You wouldn't have his last address, would you?"

"Just a minute." After a long pause, he said, "205 Carter Street . . . it's an apartment in Glendale."

"I appreciate it."

"No problem. Have you got a part for him?"

"I think he just played the biggest part of his career."

"How's that?"

"Nothing. Actually, this is more of a personal matter."

"Well, when you see him, tell him old Milt said hello."

"I will."

It was clever and thoughtful of Leigh to have arranged for my tailor to ready some clothes for me. I went through the articles that Lou had delivered. They were very stylish. I selected a pale yellow dress shirt to go with the brown trousers and the beige sports coat—all a perfect fit. The loafers were also my size. I dressed and slipped my .38 under the waistband at the middle of my back. I then waited for nightfall and drove to Glendale.

The map I checked in the telephone directory pinpointed the exact location of Carter Street, and after one wrong turn, I pulled up to the curb in the 200 block, just two doors down from Tracy's address. It was a modest area. Even under the forgiving shadows engendered by the weak glow of the street lamps, I could tell that the series of two-story brick apartments had seen better days. The front yards were a little patchy; the sidewalks that led to each unit were cracked and crumbling. Except for a kid sitting on a curb listening to an iPod, there was no activity in the neighborhood.

I left the jeep and walked to the unit at the end of the block. The front door was unlocked, and I entered the building's dimly lit foyer, where my nostrils were immediately assaulted by the stale odor of cigarette smoke. A television was blaring from one apartment. It sounded as though someone was listening to Custer's Last Stand. Half a dozen mailboxes had residents' names affixed to them, and I quickly found L. TRACY on one of them. I walked up a flight of stairs that creaked beneath my weight and made my way down a narrow hallway until I reached the last door on the right. I pressed my ear against the door, but I heard nothing inside. I knocked lightly and waited. There was no answer. I tried the knob but found it locked. I was ready to try one of my picks when a voice came from over my shoulder.

"He's not in."

I turned suddenly, surprised to see a woman standing in the doorway of the apartment across the way. She was about forty, on the short side but stoutly built. She wore a light-colored cotton print dress and slippers. Her bleached blond hair, which was dark at the roots, hung loosely at her shoulders.

"Do you know when he'll be back?"

She shrugged as she took a long drag on her cigarette.

"How long has he been gone?"

"A couple of days."

I walked over to her. "It's important that I contact him."

She struck a casual pose as she leaned against the door frame. "You a cop?" she asked, staring at me narrowly, smoke curling up her face.

"No."

"I've never seen you around here before."

"I've never been here before."

"There hasn't been anybody looking for Larry in quite a while."

"His agent might have something for him. I was asked to contact him."

She chuckled. "You'd have to dry him out first."

"Well, I wouldn't know anything about that. I'm just delivering a message."

"What's it worth to you to find him?"

I considered her for a moment. Then I reached into my pocket and handed her a twenty.

She took it and stuffed it down the front of her dress. "Larry's unpredictable. Sometimes he's gone for days at a time. I don't know where he goes, but he's got a friend—a stripper named Mona Graves. She does an act at The King's Castle. You know the joint?"

"I know it."

"Hmm, that's surprising."

"How's that?"

"You look like you got class. Nobody with any class would go to a dump like that."

"Looks can be deceiving."

She ran her eyes up and down me until I felt naked standing before her. "I don't think so. Not in your case, handsome."

"Thanks."

"You wanna come in for a while? I got some bourbon."

"Maybe another time."

She shrugged. "Suit yourself. The door's always open. Good luck finding the lush." She stepped back into her apartment and closed the door.

The King's Castle was a second-rate strip joint operated by an ex-Army staff sergeant named Westy King. I had crossed paths with him years ago when I was searching for a wayward teen who happened to be working for him. There was a bad scene, and Westy's license was pulled for a few months. He'd never viewed me in a favorable light after that, but I didn't lose any sleep over the incident.

I parked in an alley a block away from King's establishment and strolled past a couple of winos rummaging through a Dumpster. They failed to take notice of me, as they were lost in their own world.

The street was ill-lit. The neighborhood was a smattering of liquor stores, pawnshops, and bars. The sidewalks were littered and dirty. An idler wearing a leather jacket and sporting multiple piercings leaned against the door of an abandoned store. His eyes were glazed as he stared at me vacantly. I walked past him and stood under the marquee of The King's Castle. The front of the establishment was glitzy and glaring with flashing lights and brightly painted signs. Several life-sized posters offered glimpses of statuesque women in revealing costumes of the medieval period. Their names reflected the theme of the era—Lady Guinevere, Lancelot's Lusty Lady, Goody Knight. As soon as I entered, a young man in a tux assessed me a cover charge. I paid him and negotiated my way down a short flight of stairs to a dimly lit room. Ten or twelve tables filled the center, strategically positioned in front of a stage, from which a short runway extended into the audience. As the name of the establishment suggested, the motif was a castle. Suits of armor stood on each side of the stage. Waitresses dressed in diaphanous tunics and tights hustled back and forth, carrying drinks to some twenty or thirty customers. A pair of balconies in the design of turrets projected from above, where an overflow of customers could be seated. At the moment, they were unoccupied. I'd always thought that Westy King was too wrapped up in his own name. Off to the left was a bar that seated about a dozen. There were only three or four patrons drinking at present.

As I headed toward the bar, I hoped that Westy King was not on the premises. Not only would he recognize me, but he would not hesitate to blow the whistle on me in return for past favors. I slid onto a stool and asked for a beer. A short bartender with a pencil-thin mustache, small dark eyes, and large ears nodded and filled a glass for me. I paid him and turned around as I heard music. It came from a three-piece band in the pit to the right of the stage. A shapely redhead soon emerged from behind the curtains and started a slinky saunter across the stage amid a smattering of wolf whistles and applause. She wore an elaborately decorated floor-length gown with full sleeves and a conical hat from which dangled a thin wisp of silk.

"Is that Goody Knight?" I asked.

The bartender shook his head. "Nah, that's Lady Guinevere. She's the boss' personal property."

"By the boss, you mean Westy King?"

"That's right."

"I thought I saw him when I first arrived."

"Not tonight, you didn't, buddy. Mr. King had a tooth pulled. He's home nursing it with a bottle of scotch."

I nodded, secretly relieved for one break anyway. I sipped my beer for a few minutes while I watched Lady Guinevere begin her routine. She seemed well received by an audience of mostly over-the-hill gents who leered at her as though in a trance. Finally, I motioned for the bartender.

"I'd like to have a word with Mona Graves. Is she performing tonight?"

"Who?" he asked, seeming confused.

"Mona Graves."

"Oh, you mean Maid Marian. You just missed her number."

"That's too bad. Is it possible for me to talk to her?"

"Sorry, buddy. No fraternizing between the performers and the clientele. House rules."

I reached into my pocket and pulled out some bills. I put one on the bar in front of him.

He started to reach for it but shook his head.

"I only need five minutes of her time. Strictly business, I can assure you," I added, laying another bill on top of the first.

He glanced around nervously and then slid the bills across the bar and slipped them into his pocket. "Past the bar, through that curtain, second door on the right. Wait until the drumroll. That's when the lights dim."

I had another sip of my beer and waited. At the designated moment, I took my cue, moving toward the curtain amid a sudden roar from the audience. I slipped into a long corridor lit by a few low-watt bulbs and an exit light. When I reached the second door, I knocked softly. After a pause, I heard a woman's voice say, "Come in."

I opened the door and entered a small room with a sofa, an easy chair, and a dressing table covered with notions. Off to my left were several costumes hanging from a rack, and beyond that was the open door to a bathroom. A divider, on which were draped several garments, stood next to the bathroom. Just above the divider, I saw the head of a woman.

"Well, hello," she said in a mellow tone as she moved around the divider, fastening the belt on her floor-length silk gown.

"Miss Graves?"

"That's right," she replied, measuring me closely with her eyes. She was easily forty, with blond hair, fair features, and nicely sloped shoulders. Her robe was open at the bottom, where a well-turned leg protruded. "I generally have to fumigate the premises after most of my visitors leave, but you're a breath of fresh air."

"Thank you."

"What's your pleasure, honey?"

"I'm looking for Lawrence Tracy."

Her eyes immediately narrowed, and she placed her hands on her hips in a defiant pose. "I might've known. A good-looking guy with class enters my dressing room, and he happens to be looking for somebody else—and a man to boot. What makes you think I'm his keeper?"

"One of his neighbors suggested you might know how to reach him."

"Oh, and I'll bet I know which one of his neighbors—that over-the-hill bimbo. That no-good liar!"

I shifted uneasily on my feet.

"Who are you, anyway?"

"I'm working for an agent who might have a part for Tracy."

"Oh, really! Do you expect me to believe that? Larry hasn't had a part in over a year."

"Actually, I think he has."

"What do you mean by that?"

"Did Larry ever mention someone named Manny Gorzik?"

"No."

"What about Bendix?"

She did not respond to my question. She did not have to. Her eyes betrayed her.

"I don't know where Larry is," she said, turning away. "I haven't seen him in weeks."

"Is there any way that you can think of that I can get in touch with him?"

"No."

"It's very important. I'd be willing to pay to find him."

"I don't sell out my friends."

Just then, the door opened, and a large, heavyset man stepped in. He had dark curly hair, a nose that looked as though it had once been broken, and a square jaw.

"What is it? What do you want, Crumpler? How dare you enter my dressing room without knocking?"

"You know the rules, baby. No male visitors in the dressing rooms. It gives the club a bad name," he said as he leveled his eyes on me.

"There isn't much that could give this dump a bad name," she returned.

"It isn't her fault. I was leaving, anyway," I replied.

"Glad to hear it. But you'll be leavin' with a few bruises, just so's you remember not to come back."

"There's no need for that. He's a gentleman. He even called me Miss Graves."

"You'd best step outside into the hall, Mona. This 'gentleman's' about to learn some new manners."

He took a step toward me, and I backed away.

Grinning, he said, "There's no place to hide, mister. You might as well make it easy on yourself."

When I felt my right heel touch the baseboard behind me, I knew exactly how much room I had in which to maneuver. As soon as I saw him crouch and lean, I knew he was left-handed. He came up quickly with a hard, driving punch that I barely averted. His fist struck the wall behind me, leaving a dent the size of a dinner plate. I countered with a pair of jabs to his midsection and then moved away toward the center of the room. He turned around and faced me, panting hard as he clutched his side, glaring at me with hard rage.

"I'm on my way out," I said, moving backward toward the door.

"Oh, you ain't goin' yet. Your lesson is just about to start."

Mona screamed as he lunged for me, his arms outstretched, his huge hands angling toward my throat.

I swung my leg up in a short arc, catching him squarely in the stomach with the toe of my shoe. A rush of air escaped from his lungs as he doubled over in pain. I then struck him a solid blow to the base of his neck. He dropped like a sack of wet cement and did not stir again.

Straightening my coat, I turned to Mona. "I'm sorry. I hope you won't get into any trouble over this."

"I can take care of myself, but you'd better go. Mr. King has other goons on the premises."

"All right, I'll leave, but if you see Tracy, tell him that he's in trouble—big trouble."

"What do you mean?" she asked, taking a step forward.

"Just that he's involved in a murder . . . maybe two."

"No, Larry would never do anything like that. He'd never hurt anyone," she uttered, a frightened expression on her face.

My gut reaction told me that I should believe her.

"Maybe, maybe not. It's possible he doesn't even know what he's gotten himself into, but he's in it either way—up to his neck—and there's only one way to get him out of it. He's got to go to the police."

"The police?"

"I'm afraid there's no other way."

The color all but drained from her face as she stared at me.

Twenty minutes later, a cab pulled up to the side entrance of The King's Castle. Thirty seconds after that, Mona Graves emerged and hustled into it. I followed at a discreet distance. After a short drive, the cab came to a stop in front of a modest brick home with a small front yard. Mona left the vehicle and disappeared inside. I parked half a block away, killed my headlights, and waited. Within seconds I saw a light go on in the house. I waited a few more minutes and then left the jeep and walked down the sidewalk. I stepped around to the side of the house and tried to catch a glimpse inside. Unfortunately, the drapes were drawn on every window. By the time I worked my way back to the front of the house, I could hear a woman crying. I thought I heard the voice call out the name Larry, but I could not be sure. I rang the bell. After a long pause, the door opened, and Mona stood in front of me in tears.

"There's something wrong with Larry. He needs help," she muttered.

I pushed past her and entered a small living room, where I saw a man sprawled out on a sofa. On the coffee table and on the floor beside him were several overturned bottles. I approached him and knelt down. He was turned away from me, and I moved his head around to get a look at his face. His eyes were closed, his skin was ashen, and his mouth drooped open. From his present appearance, it was difficult to determine if he were the same man who had presented himself to me as Richard Armitage. Nevertheless, the facial structure and the prominent nose gave me the impression that he was. I felt his wrist but could detect no pulse. I placed my head against his chest. There was no heartbeat.

"What is it? What's wrong with him?" Mona asked, desperation in her voice. "Why won't he come to?"

"He's gone, Mona."

"No, he can't be! Larry always drank too much—I've told him that many times—but he's never had so much that it would kill him."

I picked up one of the bottles and sniffed it. "It wasn't the amount that he drank."

"What do you mean?"

I held the bottle to her nose. Her eyes widened as she took a sniff.

"Where did he get this?"

She did not respond. She merely stared blankly at the man on the sofa.

I took her by the arms and shook her. "The scotch—where did he get it?"

"I . . . I don't know . . . I'm not sure," she replied in a voice that had suddenly become docile.

"Was it Bendix? Did Larry ever mention the name?"

She nodded as she stared at the floor and wrung her hands.

"What do you know about him?"

"Larry did some kind of a job for him. I don't know what exactly—some kind of acting gig. Larry got some money for his part in it. I thought that whatever the deal was, it was a good thing for Larry. It put cash in his pocket, and Bendix kept him sober—at least during the job. It wasn't until later that the scotch showed up . . . a kind of thank you, I thought, for the performance—whatever it was that Larry did."

"Did you ever meet Bendix?"

"No."

"Did Larry ever talk about him?"

"No . . . except . . ."

"Except what?"

"Well, a day or so after Larry's part was over, he said something about making some additional money—enough to make what he had already earned look like peanuts."

I nodded. "Blackmail."

"I don't understand."

"I might have been wrong about Larry. He might not have known anything about the murder Bendix planned. Larry might have just been an unwitting pawn in the whole dirty mess. But he still might have stayed alive if his greed hadn't gotten in the way."

Tears started to form in Mona's eyes.

"I want you to call Lieutenant Pete Cornell in homicide."

"Homicide?" The word seemed foreign as it came from her lips.

"That's right. Larry's been murdered. You tell Lieutenant Cornell everything you told me."

She buried her face in her hands and started to weep.

I watched her for a long moment, not knowing what I could say or do to ease her sorrow. I decided that it was something that only she could work out for herself. "I'm sorry, Mona. I won't bother you anymore."

I was rattled by Larry Tracy's death. I was also sorely disappointed. The poor loser broke the link in the chain

I was following. Bendix and Gorzik were eliminating all the loose ends and doing an excellent job of it. It seemed as though I was the only one left, and I could only wonder what they had in mind for me. Of course, they might be content to do nothing. I was already wriggling around like a worm on a hook. My ability to prove their involvement in all the deaths that had occurred was getting slimmer all the time.

I drove around aimlessly for a while, not paying much attention to what I was doing. I did not want to return directly to the bungalow, for I was tired of hiding. Besides, I thought a ride might clear my mind.

It did not. After about thirty minutes, I suddenly felt very weary. I pulled over and killed the ignition. I was exhausted—more exhausted than I'd realized—not so much from a lack of rest as from the stress that had been gnawing at me and a growing anger welling inside me. I sat in the jeep for several minutes, trying to work another angle, but I was too distracted to concentrate. There was a small cafe a block away. It was well lit and seemed to be an inviting beacon. Even better than that, at this late hour it was deserted. I decided that a strong cup of coffee might help.

I walked the short distance, seeing no one in the vicinity and feeling comfortable that I would be safe enough from being recognized. I pushed through the door and glanced around. It was inviting but empty of customers, as I had observed from the jeep. There were half a dozen booths and maybe a dozen stools at the counter. I slid onto the one nearest the door and picked up a menu.

A hefty waiter in a stained white uniform saw me, picked up a cup and saucer and a beaker of coffee, and waddled toward me.

"Coffee?" he asked.

I nodded.

"Looks like we're done with the rain," he ventured, placing a paper napkin and some utensils within my reach. His cheeks were chubby, and his face was red.

"Yeah."

"Something to eat?"

"How are the cheeseburgers?"

"The best."

"Bring me two of them—with everything."

"Any fries?"

"No."

"Right."

I watched him amble toward the kitchen window and scribble on an order form. He pinned it on a metal carousel and spun it around.

A moment later I saw a face in the kitchen window glancing at me after reading the order. I assumed he was the cook. Thick-necked and full in the face, he bore a strong resemblance to the waiter except that he was bald.

I poured some sugar into my coffee and mixed it. I took a sip. It was as strong as I thought it would be and felt bracing going down. I quickly drained the rest of the cup. I could feel the muscles in my neck and shoulders starting to relax. I lowered my head and pressed my fingers against my eyes. For a long moment, I was lost in thought. I did not even notice the waiter approach me until I heard him refilling my cup.

"How'd you like the coffee?"

"It's just what I needed."

"Tough day?"

"Very tough."

He regarded me closely. "Your burgers will be out in a few minutes."

I nodded.

Five minutes later, I heard a door open. I looked up and was surprised to see the cook standing in the kitchen doorway.

"Take it easy, mister. We don't want any trouble," the waiter said as he stepped around the counter and stood next to me.

"What is this?"

"We know who you are. Your picture's been in all the papers. We've also seen you on TV. You're the private peeper who's wanted for murdering that writer."

"You're wrong. I didn't kill anyone."

He grinned. "Nope. You're the one, all right. The cops are on the way. We figure there's bound to be some kind of reward for you."

Slowly, I slipped off the stool.

The cook took a step toward me and raised a hand. I was stunned to see a cleaver in it.

"Take it easy," the waiter said. "We don't want to hurt you. We just want to hold you here until the boys in blue arrive."

In the distance I could hear police sirens.

I sidestepped toward the end of the counter. As I did, the waiter moved toward me, reaching for me with his beefy hands. Just as he was about to encircle me with his arms, I ducked and slipped around behind him. He started to turn, and I helped him, grabbing his arm and, taking advantage of his size and momentum, steering him into the cook. I heard the collision, followed by some swearing, but I did not linger, for I was already behind the counter making a dash for the kitchen door.

"Stop him, Wiley!"

Glancing over my shoulder, I saw the cook raise the cleaver and fling it. I ducked behind the counter and watched as the blade embedded itself in the wall.

I raced into the kitchen, which was littered with cardboard boxes and cylindrical containers. I spotted the back door and ran for it. In my haste, I tripped and bumped into some dishes stacked on a shelf, knocking them over with a shattering sound. The door was unlocked, and I burst through it. I found myself in an alley lined with trash bins. I decided to go to my right. My decision proved to be a bad one. At the end of the passage was an eight-foot-high chain-link fence. I paused and decided to retreat, but the sirens were now very close. They seemed to be coming from different directions. A dog started to bark somewhere nearby. I took a running start and made for the fence. It was not easy, but I managed to scale it without busting a gut, straddled the top, swung my trailing leg over, and then let myself drop. I hit the pavement on the opposite side and continued to move.

Five minutes later, after racing down another alley and some backyards, I managed to double back toward the jeep. I could see the flashing lights atop a pair of squad cars parked in front of the cafe. I saw the waiter standing near the door waving his arms dramatically. While two officers were taking his statement, two others were moving around the building with flashlights.

I felt confident that the waiter had not seen me arrive in the jeep. In that regard, I considered that I could simply drive away, and that was exactly what I did.

Chapter Seven

It was half past one, and I had not yet heard from Leigh. She was always prompt. If she had been delayed for any reason, she would have contacted me. I began to worry. I decided to give her another fifteen minutes. If by then she did not make contact, I would make my way to a pay phone and call the office first, her cell phone next.

Ten minutes later, I heard a car pull into the driveway. I peeked through the curtains. It was Leigh. She was in Margie's blue Buick. I opened the back door, and she quickly stepped in, a worried expression on her face.

"Leigh, you're late. I was getting concerned."

She shook her head. "Lieutenant Cornell dropped by the office. He was lecturing me again for half an hour. He knows we've been in contact with each other. He wants you to turn yourself in in the worst way."

"I know he does. I'm sorry about the tongue-lashing."

"Then I had a hard time losing his plainclothesman. I went to Barney's diner and left through the window in the ladies' room. Margie let me borrow her car. It was the only way I could shake the tail."

"Did you see who it was?"

"It looked like Sergeant Drysdale."

"The one who keeps asking you out?"

She rolled her eyes. "I can't stand him. I hope he's still back at the diner."

I smiled.

"I also spotted someone else who I thought was tailing me—near my home."

"Did you recognize him?"

"It was a she—some blond in a gray Mercury—and no, I didn't recognize her."

"Hmm."

"John, I don't think I'm going to be able to get away with this again. They're starting to put the pressure on."

"We'll talk about that later." I pulled out a chair for her, and I sat down opposite her. "What exactly is eating Cornell?"

"John, did you go to the florist's shop yesterday to see Myron Bendix as you planned?"

"I saw him. I didn't get anywhere with him."

"And after that, did you come right back here?"

"I did for a while. Then I finally remembered where I had heard the voice of the man who'd impersonated Armitage. He was a small-time local actor named Lawrence Tracy. I managed to trace him through a stripper named Mona Graves." Quickly, I briefed her on the events of the previous evening.

She listened closely to every word. Finally, she asked, "What time did you finally get back?"

"Sometime around eleven-thirty, I suppose. Why? Why all the questions?"

"Joe Bendix was found murdered last night. The approximate time of death was between ten and midnight."

I stared at her blankly as I attempted to digest her words.

"Lieutenant Cornell knows that you saw Myron Bendix yesterday. Myron told him that you were in his shop making inquiries about Joe. He said that you were hostile, that you made accusations concerning his brother, and that he ordered you off the premises."

"I wasn't exactly 'hostile,' but the rest is more or less true."

"Lieutenant Cornell also spoke to Mona Graves. She told him about your visit, although she claimed she didn't know your name."

"She didn't. I never told her my name."

"It took the lieutenant all of thirty seconds to put you at the scene. Mona told him that you accused Bendix of poisoning Lawrence Tracy. She said that you claimed that Bendix had involved Tracy in some kind of plot."

I nodded. "And Bendix gets bumped off just a matter of hours after I bad-mouthed him in front of two witnesses."

"That's about the size of it. You didn't go anywhere

near Joe Bendix, did you, John?" she asked, her eyes pleading.

"No, Leigh, I didn't."

She breathed a sigh of relief. "I thought maybe you might have gotten frustrated and decided to confront him, and that things might have turned ugly."

"No. I wouldn't have gone anywhere near Joe Bendix while he was under police surveillance. Speaking of which, he was under surveillance, wasn't he?"

"Yes."

"And he was still murdered?"

"There was a plainclothesman parked in front of his house, but he was only there to monitor Bendix's movements. The police had no reason to suspect that Bendix himself was in any danger."

"Did they determine how the killer gained access?"

"Lieutenant Cornell found evidence that an intruder entered through the rear door of the garage and then forced his way in through the kitchen door."

"And then left the same way, no doubt?"

"Apparently."

"How was Bendix killed?"

"His neck was broken."

"I see."

"That sounds like the way your wrestler friend might dispose of someone. Do you think they had a falling-out?"

"Could be. What about Gorzik? Wasn't he under surveillance as well?"

"Yes. The officer at that scene reported that the lights were on in his house, and he appeared to remain at home, but it's possible that he slipped out the back. He could have killed Bendix and returned without anyone knowing for certain."

I nodded, lost in thought.

She stared at me in silence as I considered everything she told me. Finally, she said, "What do you think?"

I smiled at her. "I think you look nice in that lavender dress. Is it new?"

"Boss, be serious. You're now officially a suspect in multiple murders."

"Well, they can only execute me once."

"Please, don't be morbid."

"By the way, did you learn anything about Henry Waller?"

"Not much. Lieutenant Cornell said he was a widower. He lived alone. According to his neighbors, he worked as a caretaker. It looks as though he might have been employed by the Martinsons, who, by the way, are on an extended European vacation."

"The owners of the home in Santa Monica."

"That's right. Nothing has been confirmed yet, but Lieutenant Cornell is attempting to reach them."

"All right. Whatever part Waller might have had in this, if any, is over now."

Leigh placed her hands on the table palms down. "Are you going to turn yourself in to Lieutenant Cornell?"

"No."

"Maybe it's time."

"Somebody has murdered four people. As you pointed out, I'm the likely candidate for at least two of those murders. I thought I had all the answers until Joe Bendix was killed. Now, I'm not so sure."

"But don't you think Manny Gorzik was responsible for that?"

"Maybe. I don't know. I just have to learn more of the facts before I turn myself in. I have to find a hook."

She nodded. "I'll continue to play it your way. Whatever you want, I'll be there for you."

I placed my hands on top of hers, and our fingers interlocked. "I know you will, but it's best that you avoid coming here again. Up until now, we've been lucky. Our luck can't hold much longer."

"All right. From here on, I'll just stay in touch by pay phone."

"Agreed."

"What's our next move?"

"How about some chili?"

"What!"

"Lou brought some of Barney's chili over when he dropped by. I'm hungry. How about you?"

She smiled. "I'll fix it."

After Leigh left, I sat down to think things through. There seemed to be only one person of interest left in this melodrama, and that was Manny Gorzik. Since he would not benefit financially from the deaths of Richard Armitage or Joe Bendix, it stood to reason that the only remaining motivation for his actions was revenge against me. If that were the case, he already appeared to have succeeded. I was a suspect in several murders, on the lam, with a tall mountain to climb in order to clear myself. There was nothing else he had to do but sit back and watch me squirm; yet something in the back of my mind told me that there was a sour note in all this. I had gotten to know Gorzik pretty well while I was investigating the armored-car case in which he was involved. He was no rocket scientist. It was obvious that this entire scene was not of Manny Gorzik's design. He lacked the refinement and the ability to orchestrate any of this. There had to have been a mutual accord between him and Joe Bendix with the combined goals of money and revenge. Now, with Joe Bendix dead, the ball was in Gorzik's court. And multiple homicides and especially this waiting game was just not his style. There was a simple directness about him that I had come to understand. Gorzik would prefer to rip off my arm or stomp on me until I was a bloody pulp, but what was he waiting for? With Bendix no longer pulling his strings, why wasn't he just confronting me in an alley somewhere?

I poured myself another cup of coffee and turned on the local news. Once again, my picture flashed across the screen. This time, it was in connection with the death of Joe Bendix. The newscaster indicated the relationship between the deceased and Richard Armitage. Two plus two

equaled my guilt. Captain Morelli, Pete Cornell's imme-
diate superior, then made an appearance, flanked by Pete
and some other high-ranking officials. They issued a few
pat statements before Pete stepped to the microphone. He
struck his stern, official police pose and answered a few
questions from the media. During the Q-and-A session, I
was referred to as a "person of interest" in conjunction
with both murders. Pete offered only scant details, indicating that he could not comment further on an ongoing
investigation.

The entire segment was disheartening. I had to admit
that I looked bad. I was looking even worse by the day because I refused to turn myself in. I began to doubt myself.
Maybe Leigh was right. Perhaps I should just walk into
Pete's office and throw my cards onto the table. After all,
what more could I do now? Every lead that I'd pursued
had turned up dead. Manny Gorzik was the only remaining link, and I was beginning to wonder if I knew him
as well as I thought I did. Maybe prison had changed his
way of thinking. Was it possible that he was now content
with tearing down my reputation and forcing me into
hiding instead of physically tearing me apart as he had
threatened? I decided to sleep on it one more night. In the
morning, unless I could come up with a fresh approach, I
would call Pete and turn myself in.

When the telephone rang, I stirred uneasily. A glance
at my watch told me that it was just past midnight. Warily, I picked up the receiver and said, "Yeah?"

"Hello, Hazard."

I recognized the voice at once and immediately sat up in bed. It was Manny Gorzik.

"Well, Manny, I expected to hear from you sooner. What took you so long?"

"I had business to take care of."

"So I've heard. You've been a busy boy."

He chuckled.

"It's time the two of us got together."

"You're readin' my mind, Hazard."

"Set the time and the place."

"Uh-uh. It's not goin' to work that way. This time, I'm dealin'."

"Then why did you bother to wake me up in the middle of the night?"

"I wanted to give you time to make out your will." He laughed dryly and then added, "You'll be hearin' from me."

"Look, you buffoon—"

I heard a click, and the line went dead.

I lay down again and thought about what he'd said. It was Gorzik, all right—there was no doubt about it—but somehow he had changed. The bull in the china shop had become a different man. I did not get it. Unless . . . I sat up suddenly and threw off my covers. How had he gotten my number? There could have been only one way: Leigh. I quickly dialed her number. After eight rings, there was still no answer, and no voice mail either.

Five minutes later, I was dressed and in the jeep. Staying within the speed limit to avoid being pulled over by any patrol cars, I managed to make the half-hour drive to Leigh's house in twenty-five minutes, thanks in part to the light traffic at so late an hour. Remembering that Leigh was still under surveillance, I parked on the next street and worked my way through her neighbor's driveway and backyard until I reached Leigh's property. I knelt down among some oleander bushes and scanned her house and the entire yard for any activity. There was none. Everything was dark and quiet. I was familiar with the layout of Leigh's home, for I had helped her move in and was a regular at her Halloween and Christmas parties. I knew that Leigh kept a spare key under the second planter from the door on her patio. I hurried to it, located it, and opened her back door without hesitation. My .38 in my hand, I entered and quietly closed the door behind me. I froze where I was for a full minute, straining to hear any noise or detect any movement, but I sensed nothing. Cautiously, I moved forward, inching my way down the narrow hallway, with which I was familiar. Even so, I nearly walked into a small table, catching myself barely in time. Leigh's bedroom was the second door on the right, just past her den. I noticed that her bedroom door was open, but the room was dark. I moved forward slowly and peeked inside. The drapes on her window were partly open, and there was just enough light to tell me that her bed had not been slept in. I flipped on the light switch. At the foot of her bed was a nightgown she'd probably been planning to wear. Next to it was the phone receiver, off the hook, accounting for the endless ringing on her call-waiting. The closet door was open. I walked over and took a look inside. The hangers were scrambled, and most of her clothes appeared to be missing—definitely not Leigh's usual, organized style.

It took me only three minutes to check the rest of the house. I found nothing unusual and no sign of forced entry.

Where was the surveillance unit? It was time for me to face the music. I couldn't leave Leigh in jeopardy. I stepped out onto the front porch and looked up and down the street. There was a white van parked at the curb in front of the house next door. Across the street, about fifty feet away, was a dark two-door. I guessed that that was it. I hustled over to it and approached the driver's side. There was a man inside, slumped over on the front seat. I opened the door and examined him. There was a slight cut on his head just above the left temple, where a bruise was forming. I placed my finger against his neck and felt a pulse. It was strong; apparently, he was just knocked out. I pulled his ID from his wallet. His name was Les Adams. He was a sergeant. I reached for his radio transmitter and called in. Within seconds, a dispatcher's voice crackled over the air. I announced that an officer had been injured and required medical attention. I gave his name and provided Leigh's address. When the dispatcher asked me to identify myself, I replaced the transmitter and left. I was back in the jeep and two blocks away when I heard the blaring sound of a siren approaching from the opposite direction.

My ride back to the bungalow was a grim one. Leigh was in trouble, maybe even dead. No, it was unlikely that she was dead. If Gorzik had wanted her dead, he would have killed her right there in her own home. No, he wanted her for another reason. She was his bargaining chip, and he was dealing now . . . all the way. He was dealing, and he had all the cards, and I knew it, only I was too late to see it coming. I was still being played. There was nothing more for me to do but wait for him to contact me again. Soon, very soon, Gorzik would call. Of that, I had no doubt.

I slept little the rest of the evening, worrying about Leigh and feeling guilty over my failure to anticipate her abduction. If I had turned myself in to the police, Leigh would be safe and asleep in her bed right now.

I arose early and turned on the television in the hope of hearing something about Leigh's disappearance. There was nothing on at the five o'clock hour or at five-thirty, but on the six o'clock report, there was finally a mention. A camera crew was on the scene at Leigh's house, where a reporter stood on the sidewalk announcing the assault on the officer who had been maintaining surveillance on her. He went on to identify Leigh as my secretary and reminded the viewing audience of my fugitive status in connection with the death of the renowned writer, Richard Armitage. Several theories were set forth, including the possibility that I was the one who had overpowered the officer and that Leigh was now on the run with me. I shook my head in disgust as the newsman closed his report and the network returned to the studio anchors.

I made myself some scrambled eggs, toast, and coffee as I attempted to reason things out, but my innermost thoughts kept returning to Leigh. Finally, I headed for the jeep and drove to the nearest pay phone.

The LAPD dispatcher patched me through to Pete Cornell, who seemed both surprised and angry to hear from me.

"I told you before, and I'll tell you again—come in now."

"He's got Leigh, Pete."

Immediately, his voice changed. "Who's got her?"

"Manny Gorzik."

"Are you sure?"

"No, but he telephoned me early this morning at a number that only Leigh knows."

There was a long pause on the other end.

"Pete, are you there?"

"Do you know that Captain Morelli believes that Leigh is with you now?"

"That's ridiculous."

"Is it? She's gone. Most of her clothes are missing. There was no forced entry, no signs of violence. As far as the LAPD is concerned, the two of you are on the run."

"You mean as far as Captain Morelli is concerned. The only reason he's a captain is because of his brother-in-law, and you know it."

"She's your loyal secretary. Everybody knows that she'd do anything for you. She certainly hasn't played ball with us."

"Tell Captain Morelli to get his head out of the sand."

"Do you know that we've gotten reports from concerned citizens who have sighted you everywhere from Gardena to Santa Barbara? Now we're getting calls from people who have reported seeing the two of you together."

"For the last time, Leigh is not with me."

"John, you should come in."

"Do me a favor."

"I don't do favors for fugitives—even when they're friends of mine."

"Then don't do it for me. Do it for Leigh."

There was a long pause. For a moment, I thought the line went dead.

"Pete?"

"I'm here."

"Mona Graves."

"The stripper?"

"That's right. Find out what kind of car she drives."

"Why?"

"Leigh told me she thought she was being tailed by a blond in a gray Mercury. That doesn't sound like anyone in your department."

"It isn't." He paused again for a long moment. "You think Mona's deeper in this than it appears?"

"She's the only blond I know who's connected with anybody on this case."

"All right," he finally said grudgingly, "and while I'm at it, I'll check on the latest whereabouts of one Manny Gorzik."

"I'll call you back in an hour."

When I had Pete on the line again, he deflated my balloon.

"Mona doesn't own a car. She never has. She never learned to drive."

"No driver's license?" I said, half to myself.

"That's right. She's clean. The only thing we have on her was one arrest made about five years ago."

"For what?"

"Too much flesh, not enough feathers."

"What about her boyfriend? Maybe he has a gray Mercury."

"I'm way ahead of you. Lawrence Tracy drove an old white Cadillac, and most of the time it was in the garage. Sorry, John."

"What about Gorzik?"

"Good news and bad news."

"Let me have it."

"The bad news is that Gorzik was having a sandwich in a downtown eatery when Sergeant Adams was slugged."

"So he's got another confederate."

"Maybe."

"What's the good news?"

"We don't know where he is at the moment."

"What! That's good news?"

"Well, if your theory is right, he's probably busy laying a trap for you right now."

"I don't get it. Joe Bendix gets himself bumped off in his own home while one of your boys is parked outside, and now Manny Gorzik disappears right from under your nose. What kind of squad are you running, anyway?"

"They were under light surveillance, John. We weren't out to protect Bendix's life. We had no reason to assume he was in any danger, and we entertained no suspicions that Gorzik would take a powder. We had no proof that either one of them was involved in this matter, and we still don't. With Joe Bendix and Lawrence Tracy dead, we can't prove any connection to Armitage's murder. In fact, other than the phone call that you got from Gorzik, we still have no evidence of anything, only suspicions. Furthermore, we only have your word that Gorzik even contacted you. He could deny it."

"What about the fact that Gorzik and Bendix were in the same cell block?"

"Do you know how many cons were in the same cell block with Gorzik and Bendix for the years they were in stir? If we searched hard enough, we could probably find a few more you helped to send up. What do you suggest I do—put a twenty-four-hour watch on every one of them who gets his walking papers? Do you think I have an army of officers at my disposal?"

I took a deep breath and released it slowly. "Sorry, Pete. Thanks for what you did."

"What now?"

"I figure to get a call very soon now from Manny Gorzik."

"Don't try to handle this alone—not with that ape."

"I'll play it the way that's best for Leigh. You know that. So long, Pete. Wish me luck."

"John, you—"

I hung up the receiver.

I returned to the bungalow, where I sat down in the living room and stared at the telephone. Wild thoughts ran through my mind, visions of what might be happening to Leigh at this very moment. Had I played this caper the wrong way from the start? Maybe. I didn't know. Maybe nothing I could have done would have made any difference.

As I stared at the phone, I had an idea. I picked up the receiver and dialed Leigh's cell phone number. As I suspected, the phone was turned off, and her voice mail clicked in. I shook my head and hung up the receiver. Another dead end. I did not even know if Leigh had her cell phone with her. Besides, Pete Cornell would have already checked it out. If he had learned anything at all about her whereabouts due to her cell phone use, he would have let me know or, more likely, gone after her himself. I guessed that my logic was faulty and that I was just clutching at straws.

I passed the rest of the morning pacing the floor and staring at the phone. Nothing happened. No one called, yet I knew that it was only a matter of time.

At noon, I turned on the television again and listened to the news. Five minutes into the hour, they flashed a picture of Leigh and the same one of me. The newscaster mentioned Leigh's sudden disappearance again, but it was little more than a rehash of the earlier report. Then the newscaster, who was all blond curls and pearly teeth, started to chat with the weatherman. I turned it off and went into the kitchen to fix a pot of coffee. I was never very good at sitting around and waiting for things to happen. I had always been used to creating my own breaks, but for the life of me, I had no idea where to begin.

Finally, the call came. I had been sitting in one of the armchairs and had dozed off. The ring seemed sudden, jarring. Quickly, I reached for the receiver.

"Hazard," I said.

"John." It was Leigh's voice. She was alive. "John, don't do anything. Stay away—"

There was a pause, and then the line went dead.

"Leigh! Leigh!" I cried out as though I were trying to raise someone from the dead.

A minute later, the phone rang again. This time, it was Manny Gorzik. He spoke for about thirty seconds before hanging up without even letting me say anything. This time, when the line went dead, I did not even attempt to speak. Mechanically, I hung up the receiver as a shot of fear coursed through me—fear for Leigh and fear of my failing at being able to help her.

I sat in the darkness of the living room for a long time, trying to clear my head, attempting to assimilate the message Gorzik had just delivered. I was worried. I knew that I had to dig deep now if I were going to be able to get Leigh back. And I *had* to get Leigh back. The margin that Gorzik had left me was a narrow one. I hoped that it was not too narrow . . . for Leigh's sake. And for mine.

Chapter Eight

I was standing in the driveway next to the jeep when Barney Kennedy pulled up. He wore a grave expression as he climbed out of his pickup and shook my hand.

"Did you bring everything?" I asked.

"Yes."

We spent the next several minutes transferring items into the jeep. I locked the back door to the bungalow and started to get into the driver's seat, but Barney blocked my path.

"I'll drive. You can give me directions as we go. You'll need your strength and concentration when we get there."

I nodded and passed him the keys.

We climbed in. He started the ignition, turned on the headlights, and pulled out of the driveway. We then wound our way through the quiet streets of Newport Beach, nearly deserted at this early hour, and headed north through Santa Ana and Anaheim before turning in an easterly direction. We refueled the jeep before picking up the Interstate and began moving at a higher rate of speed.

We exchanged only a few words during the drive. I was lost in thought, and Barney respected my need for silence. The constant hum of the engine and the drone of the tires on the pavement were the only sounds I heard. The dull orbs of the headlights of oncoming cars seemed to be the only sights I noticed as they approached and then passed by us.

Several times during the drive, I found myself glancing at my watch, calculating the time I had in which to act, measuring distances in my mind, and figuring angles. I had a plan—no, more of an idea of how—to rescue Leigh, but it hinged on too many variables. The truth of the matter was that I had no idea what it was I was walking into, but it did not matter a whit. Leigh's life depended on my arrival at the time that Manny Gorzik had dictated. If I followed directions, I concluded that I had maybe one chance in ten of saving Leigh and getting out of this mess alive. If, on the other hand, I could somehow locate Leigh before that . . . well, that would be a different matter.

"What did you say the name of this place was?" Barney asked after a long silence.

"Silver Butte."

"Strange, directing you to a ghost town."

"Hmm?"

"I said, it's strange—"

"I heard you. No, it's not really that strange at all. If

you wanted to do away with someone, it's actually the ideal location. For one thing, it's isolated. No one is going to see or hear anything. For another, it's in the open. He can see us coming for miles."

"Yet it seems like something out of a Western—I mean, having a showdown with somebody on Main Street at sunup."

"Yeah, I know what you mean."

"Hazard, do you think that Leigh's really there?"

"I don't know, but I have to assume that she is."

Barney clutched the steering wheel tightly. "You realize, of course, that Leigh might be dead already. Gorzik might've killed her after he allowed her to speak to you."

I nodded. "That thought has been racing through my mind over and over again. I can only hope and pray that she's still alive. Until I know for certain one way or the other, I have no choice but to go through with this, and Gorzik knows it."

"Gorzik's holding all the cards, all right."

"Oh, I don't know. I've spent time in Silver Butte. I've been through virtually every building. At least I'm familiar with the layout of the town, and I know the general geography of the surrounding area."

"Does that give you a clue as to where he might be holding her?"

I shrugged. "She could be in half a dozen places."

Barney shook his head. Even in the dim light of the jeep, I could see how furrowed his brow was with worry.

"What do you think your chances are of finding her in the dark?"

"I wouldn't give odds, but if I can get to her and free her, then it would be a different ball game altogether."

He glanced at his watch. "We still have several hours before daylight. Maybe I should step on it. I might be able to buy you some more time—improve your odds."

I checked the green glow on the instrument panel. The needle on the speedometer measured seventy. "You're doing fine. We can't afford to get stopped by the state patrol now that we're this close."

He nodded.

The two of us fell into an uneasy silence again. I stared out the window into the blackness and considered Barney's earlier query. What would be the most likely location for Gorzik to hole up? Ever since Gorzik had called, I had been working overtime to recall the structures of Silver Butte. The livery was a good possibility. It was open and roomy. I had been too cautious to try to scale the ladder. If Gorzik could find a way to reach the loft, he would also have a commanding view of the entire vicinity. The hotel was another strong likelihood. If Gorzik positioned himself on the second floor, there would be only one way for me to reach him—the rickety staircase. There were just too many scenarios. I closed my eyes and allowed my mind to drift for a few minutes.

"That's Barstow coming up," Barney announced.

His remark brought me out of my reverie, and I took notice of the long tier of lights in the distance.

"It won't be long now."

In due time, we reached the point where I had left the Interstate on my first trip to Silver Butte. I directed Barney to abandon the pavement for the dirt road as well as to slow his speed. It was here where I made a mental note of the reading on the odometer. We drove on in silence, intent on reaching our destination and deeply preoccupied with thoughts of what lay ahead. There was a gibbous moon, and many stars were visible in the heavens. As I stared up at them, I wondered if Leigh could see them from wherever she was at this particular moment. Then I wondered again if Leigh were still alive. I decided that she was.

At the appropriate time, I signaled Barney to kill the ignition and turn off the lights. I reached over the seat and pulled out the night-vision binoculars from the backpack we had stowed earlier. We both left the jeep and walked ahead a short distance. Here, I used the binoculars to scan the land before us. At night, everything looked different, but after a minute or so, I became oriented. I recognized the outcroppings I had passed only a few days ago; I took note of the slope of the terrain; and finally I came to focus on the tor that I knew to be some eight miles away. It had been from the base of that tor that I had had my first sight of Silver Butte.

For several minutes, I swept the lenses back and forth, estimating distances and making mental calculations as to elevations. Finally, I passed the binoculars to Barney.

As he held them to his eyes, I explained my intentions. "That tor to the northeast is about as far as we can go in the jeep. Even that might be too risky, judging from the elevation. Scan toward the west . . . see those outcroppings?"

"I see them."

"If we swing just to the west of them and then back toward the northeast, we can reach a point not too distant from that tor without being seen from Silver Butte."

"I got it."

He surrendered the binoculars to me, and the two of us walked back to the jeep. He turned on the ignition again, and we moved ahead at a slower, more cautious pace. The going was smooth enough at first, but then it became very bumpy, and we had to slow down even more. Several times we had to move at a snail's pace, and on one occasion we had to back up and detour around a large cluster of rocks that lay in our path.

Eventually, we corrected our course and were back on line to reach the tor. After a time, I told Barney to pause as I pulled out the binoculars once more and scanned the landscape ahead.

"Do you think we can drive without the headlights?" I asked.

"We can try. The light is pretty good, but the ground is irregular, tricky."

"Let's try it for a while, at a slower rate of speed."

Barney nodded, and we moved ahead slowly but with definite progress as the shadow of the tor became more and more distinct with each minute. Barney handled the vehicle skillfully, with attention to the rough terrain before us. Even a slight mishap could result in a ruptured crankcase or a damaged axle. When we were within a mile or so of the tor, I instructed Barney to cut the engine. I swept the ground with the binoculars and then nodded. "This is it. We're too high now. We can't risk going any farther. I'll have to hoof it from here."

"How long will it take you to reach the town?"

"The better part of an hour . . . maybe longer."

He checked his watch. "That should put you there at least two hours before daylight."

We exited the jeep. Barney removed the backpack and set it on the hood.

"You've got water, a rope, flares, a flashlight, a .45, and extra ammo."

I hung the binoculars around my neck. I pulled the .45 from the backpack and slid it under my belt. Along with my .38, I felt pretty well heeled. I then slung the pack over my shoulders.

Barney removed his hunting rifle from the jeep and rested it against the front bumper. "If you need me, I'm just a long shot away."

I nodded. "My phone will be turned off. Keep yours on. I may use you as a diversion of some kind, or I may just need some additional firepower. I don't know yet. I'll direct you from wherever I am."

"What happens if I don't hear from you at all?"

"If I can't locate Leigh and get her out of danger, I'll

probably just have to take my chances walking down Main Street as Gorzik instructed."

Barney shook his head. "Like Gary Cooper in *High Noon,* huh?"

"Yeah, except that I don't feel very much like Gary Cooper right about now."

He smiled.

"Wait an hour after sunrise. If you haven't heard from me by then, call Pete Cornell, and have him bring in the troops."

"Right."

"Keep a good thought," I said.

We shook hands, and I turned and headed in the direction of the tor.

I walked vigorously at first, attempting to make good time, but after ten minutes, I slowed my pace, not wanting to be winded by the time I reached Silver Butte. The longer I walked, the more my eyes seemed to adjust to the darkness. The moonlight helped, and I could see for a long distance ahead of me and to my left and right. After another ten minutes, I paused and raised the binoculars to my eyes. I could see the dark outline of the buildings of Silver Butte. The town reposed in total darkness. I swept the lenses back and forth but saw nothing to indicate the presence of anyone. There was not so much as a spark of light.

I moved on, trying to determine the best way to approach. I could pick my way through the smattering of rocks and brush and head in an easterly direction for the livery. Because of its makeup, it might be the easiest building to check out. It was the tallest structure in town. If it were clear, perhaps I would attempt to reach the loft, from which I could gain a better perspective of the whole town. I could also make my way to the ravine where the stream emptied and work my way along the streambed. The elevation was a bit lower there, and I might be able to move more easily without being seen. As I walked, I reviewed the options in my mind, hoping that, for Leigh's sake, I would make the right decision.

A sudden movement off to my right startled me, and I reached for the .45 under my belt. A small rodent scurried across my path only a few feet in front of me. I took a deep breath and exhaled.

Moving again, I paused behind a clump of cholla, knelt down on one knee, and raised the binoculars to my eyes again. I was now about three hundred yards from the nearest building. The structures were still nothing but irregular shapes that were two shades darker than the skyline. I listened for any sound, for any clue that would give me an indication as to where Leigh might be, but I neither heard nor saw anything. I checked my watch. I figured I had at least an hour and a half before sunrise, yet if I failed to locate Leigh or Gorzik before then, I might just as well have wasted my efforts. I still had Barney as my ace in the hole. One idea I had been entertaining would be to have him fire off a few rounds. Perhaps the noise might induce Gorzik to show himself. Then, at least, I would have some idea as to how to advance. For the moment, I decided against it. Instead, I opted to sweep as much of the town as I could. Then, if I still met with no results, I could summon Barney.

I moved on, keeping well west of the town until I reached the ravine through which the stream passed. Here, I paused again and listened. The sound of trickling water came to my ears. I continued along the water's edge, knowing that there was no line of sight between the town and me. It gave me time to relax and reflect for a moment. I had a canteen in my backpack, but I decided to forego it for the fresh water at my feet. I knelt down, cupped my hands, and drank. It was cool and refreshing, just as I remembered it from when I had first washed in the stream. The desert, too, was cool, and yet I was sweating. I could feel beads of moisture on my brow. I took a few handfuls of water and splashed my face. It made me feel better.

I continued, following the course of the stream, which brought me closer to the town's structures. Now I could see their shapes more clearly as well as those of some of the outbuildings and several smaller, more irregular shapes that I knew to be piles of debris and boulders. Again, I swept the area with the binoculars. Nothing.

I spotted a boulder about fifty yards from the rear of the hotel. It seemed like a good place to position myself without being seen. It would also give me the closest and the best vantage point from the west side of town.

Keeping as low to the ground as possible, I covered the distance as swiftly as I could. When I reached the boulder, I knelt down and stripped off my backpack. I then sprawled out on the sand and raised the binoculars to my eyes. From here, I scanned the rear of the buildings on the west side of the main street as well as the backs of a few of the buildings on the intersecting street. At first I noticed nothing at all, until I swept the area a second time. Then, I spotted something—something that was totally out of place. I maneuvered around to the other side of the boulder to enhance my field of vision. There it was—a light-colored SUV wedged between the doctor's office and the boardinghouse on the intersecting street. It was silver, I thought, but I could not be certain. I could barely see it, but its presence told me that Gorzik was on the level and that I was expected. Now, if I only knew where he was holed up. Following several more minutes of studying each building with the binoculars, I concluded that I could learn nothing more from my present position.

I lay the binoculars on the sand beside me and attempted to recall the exact location of the buildings and their condition. High above me in the sky, I could see the flashing lights of a plane as it passed overhead, probably transporting a load of tourists to Las Vegas. I wished I could have been with them. Sipping a cold drink in a casino was a pleasant thought.

Then a coyote howled somewhere off to the north, bringing me back to the present. I pondered my next move. I decided to work my way north and check out the intersecting street and possibly even get a closer look at the SUV. I knew that once I left this spot, I would be without cover and would risk being seen by Gorzik, but as I saw it, there was no alternative. It was a calculated move but a necessary one. I could do no good remaining where I was. I wanted to push myself up to my feet, but suddenly I felt very tired. Maybe the stress of the situation was getting to me, or maybe I was just getting old. I felt the sudden urge to sleep, but I knew that I had much to do before daybreak. I decided to allow myself another minute to rest.

The desert was absolutely quiet. Its stillness magnified my sense of isolation and heightened my fear of not being able to help Leigh. It was then that I detected a slight noise—a soft padding in the sand behind me. It stopped. Then I felt something coarse clamp down on my mouth. I opened my eyes, turned slowly, and looked up.

Chapter Nine

Juniper stared down at me, holding a finger across his lips. Slowly, he removed his hand from my mouth.

"Best not speak above a whisper. Sound carries a long way in the desert," he said softly.

I nodded, relieved that I was facing my dinner companion from my first visit to Silver Butte. I pushed myself up into a sitting position. "You surely do move quietly."

Grinning, he said, "When you've been in the desert as long as I have, you become part coyote . . . and the coyote is heard only when he wants to be."

"You gave me quite a start."

"Didn't mean to." Jerking a thumb over his shoulder, he said, "Strange doin's around here lately. What's it all about?"

"There's a woman here—my secretary, in fact. She was kidnapped from her home and brought here against her will. A man is using her as bait to lure me here. I have to find her and get her to safety."

"What does this man want with you?"

"He wants to kill me."

His eyes widened, and he listened closely as I added some of the details. Finally he said, "I've seen the woman. The man with her is big—big as a mountain."

"That's him. He's a dangerous customer. Do you know exactly where they are?"

"Yep. They're in the saloon."

"The saloon. The saloon next to the mercantile, on the east side of the main street?"

"That's right. I saw them go in there yesterday just before sunset. Thought there was somethin' peculiar about the whole thing."

"There's just the two of them? Are you sure?"

"Yep."

"Not another woman—a blond?"

"Two's all I saw."

"Somehow, I've got to separate them and get the woman out of here."

He scratched his beard in thought. "That might be easier said than done."

I shook my head. "Unless I can free her before daybreak, I'll have to face him head on—on his terms."

"It don't sound too promisin' for you."

"No, it doesn't."

"Well, I don't rightly have a solution to your problem, but I can do one thing for you that might improve your odds."

"Oh?"

"I can get you closer to the rear of that saloon without bein' seen."

I listened closely.

"Remember I told you there are plenty of mine shafts around here? One of 'em runs right under the main street. It leads up the slope to the shaft east of town. You can come out there and make your way down to the back door of the saloon. Chances are, he won't be lookin' for you there."

I considered his remarks. "You're probably right . . . and that's better than nothing. Right about now, I don't have any other ideas. Let's go."

"This way."

He moved off quickly, and I followed. He headed directly toward the streambed and then altered his course to the north, where, after a walk of about a hundred yards, he stepped in front of a collection of boulders. His burro, Harry, was standing nearby, his ears twitching as we approached. Juniper pushed through some brush and stepped in front of the entrance to a shaft.

"This will take us under the street, up to the main shaft," he explained.

"Maybe you'd better wait here."

"Nope. You might not make the right turn. Won't do your lady friend any good if you end up wanderin' around in these tunnels."

He made sense. "All right, but you'd better take this," I said, pulling the .45 from my belt.

He took it and turned it over in his hands. "Haven't seen one of these since Vietnam."

"You were in Vietnam?"

"Yep."

"You'll have to tell me about it—if we get out of this."

"Glad to," he said, tucking the weapon under his belt. He took a step toward the shaft, but I stopped him.

An idea suddenly struck me. If I could signal Barney at the appropriate moment to approach the main street of Silver Butte, I could divert Gorzik's attention, possibly even get him to leave the saloon long enough for me to enter and get Leigh out of harm's way. Barney could remain in the jeep at a safe distance from the saloon, keeping out of direct danger from Gorzik. I decided I had better make my call now, for once I entered the shaft, I doubted I would be able to generate any transmission. "Just a minute, Juniper. I have to make a call first."

He stared at me as I pulled out my cell phone and dialed Barney. Barney's voice came across, and I quickly told him about my contact with Juniper, explained my situation, and outlined my plan. When I finished, there was a brief pause. Then Barney acknowledged and indicated he would be ready if and when I needed him.

"You got any more friends out there?" Juniper asked.

"He's the only one in the area, but he's as good a backup as anyone needs."

"That's good to know. I heard your plan."

"What do you think?"

"It's hard tellin'. This man holdin' your lady friend—I suppose it all depends on the kind of man he is."

"He can be a little crazy at times."

Juniper shook his head.

"Yeah."

He turned toward the shaft. "There's a lantern in here somewhere."

"We won't need one," I replied, pulling out my flashlight and handing it to him.

He took it, flipped it on, and shined the bright beam down the mouth of the shaft. Grinning, he said, "This is mighty handy. The old boys who worked these mines could've used one of these back when Silver Butte was lively."

"I imagine so."

He stepped into the shaft, and I followed at his heels.

The light bounced off the walls of the ancient shaft, revealing dark rock with specks that glistened under the beam. The dirt floor muffled our tread as we kicked up soft clouds of dust with each step.

Juniper moved ahead of me with a certitude that testified to his familiarity with the tunnels, turning once and then a second time at the intersections of shafts before finally pausing. He passed the beam of the flashlight across the ceiling of the shaft, where cobwebs clung at odd angles to the wooden shoring. Turning to me, he said, "We're under the main street of Silver Butte right about now."

"Is this timber safe?" I asked.

He shrugged. "It's been here more than a hundred years, but you never can tell. Could last another century, or it could go at any time."

His remark did little to comfort me as I eyed the shaft ahead warily.

We progressed another fifty feet or so before we reached a wooden ladder. Here, Juniper passed the flashlight to me while he picked up a lantern and lit it. Its soft glow somehow made me feel a bit more alive as I cast my eyes around me. We appeared to be in a section of the shaft that was larger than usual—about eight feet by ten, I estimated. Off to one side was a pile of ore about five feet high. Next to it were some shattered timbers that leaned against one wall.

I watched Juniper as he held the lantern over his head. "This is the end of this level. From here, we go up," he announced.

I nodded. "Amazing that that lantern still works after all these years."

"Shucks, this lantern isn't more than five years old."

"How can you tell?"

"I bought it myself in a hardware store in Barstow."

I shook my head. "You've spent a lot of time in these mines, haven't you?"

"Son, I'm a prospector. Abandoned or not, this was still once a working silver mine. Even though it played out, that doesn't mean there isn't hope that just below the surface, lightning won't strike again. Every prospector has to check out those possibilities."

I conceded that he had a point.

"It's true I've spent many an hour down here. Never found enough silver to fill a thimble, but you never know."

He hung the lantern from a peg and started to scale the ladder. It creaked loudly under his weight.

"You think this will hold me?" I asked.

"Only one way to find out."

He climbed halfway up and then turned to look down at me. "Tuck the flashlight into that pack of yours. We can use it once we reach the next level."

I did as he directed. I watched him climb to the top and move off the ladder before I placed my foot on the lowest rung. He bent over, put his hands on his knees, and looked down at me. Seeing me hesitate, he said, "Well, come ahead. If you fall, you won't go that far."

Cautiously, I began my ascent. The wood felt rotten to me, and as I climbed, I was prepared for it to collapse at any second, but I continued nevertheless. It creaked loudly with each move I made, but, surprisingly, I reached the top and felt considerable relief when I finally stepped off the old wooden structure.

"I told you it would hold," he said, grinning. "Now, let me have that flashlight again."

I did as he instructed. He took the flashlight and set off again with me trailing behind. We assumed what I imagined to be a northerly direction, passing still another intersecting shaft that dead-ended in a cave-in about ten feet inside. Finally, we came across some rails that ran along the floor. These, we followed for a short distance before encountering some old picks, some broken-down machinery that I did not recognize, and a mound of debris, against which lay an overturned ore cart. Sidestepping our way around these obstacles, we covered another fifty feet or so before we reached the main entrance to the mine. Here we stopped and looked through the boards that had been nailed across the passageway. It had not been so long ago that I had stood on the opposite side and peered in during my first visit to Silver Butte. In the distance, just over the mountains, the first rays of sunlight were beginning to penetrate the darkness of the night sky. In another twenty minutes or so, it would be light. I could see the outline of the buildings below, a shade darker than the skyline. Concentrating on the spot where I knew the saloon to be, I was already able to pick out several dark shapes behind it.

"There's a bin and some crates down near the back door of the saloon."

"Yeah, I remember."

"They're easy to trip over if you're not careful. That's your best chance. He won't be expectin' you there," Juniper explained.

I nodded, focusing on the lay of the terrain as I considered the best way to face Gorzik, providing I could even get into the saloon without alerting him. I exhaled slowly as I muttered under my breath, "I sure could use an earthquake right about now."

"How's that?" Juniper asked.

"Oh, nothing. I was just thinking aloud."

"An earthquake, you said?"

"Yeah . . . just a wild idea. It's a long story, but it might be the one way to get that man down there out into the open—away from the woman just long enough for me to get to her without endangering my friend Barney."

Juniper eyed me narrowly, probably thinking that I was crazy. "Can't create an earthquake, but I might be able to give you a tremor."

I regarded him closely, his features distorted by the glare of the flashlight in the confined space.

"What do you mean?"

He scratched his beard in thought. "Well, I could sure enough bring down a beam or two in the shaft that runs beneath the main street . . . enough to make the ground shake. It would sure enough feel like a tremor. Nobody would be able to tell the difference."

"How would you do it?"

"Explosives."

"You've got explosives?"

"Son, I'm a prospector. I've got the works right now on Harry Truman's back. Blasting caps, dynamite— everything I need for a simple job like that."

"Won't it cause a cave-in?"

"More than likely."

"I wouldn't want you to get yourself injured."

"Ha! I'll be out of the shaft feedin' sugar to Harry before the charge even goes off."

"How long will it take?"

"Half an hour—maybe less."

I smiled.

He grinned. "You work your way down to the saloon. When the charge goes off, you'll know it. After that . . . well, it's up to you and fate, I reckon."

"That it is." I extended my hand, and he took it.

"Good luck, son."

"Same to you, Juniper."

I watched him with some admiration as he disappeared down the shaft. I then turned and studied the landscape leading down to the saloon once again. I took a long look at my watch and waited. I wanted to contact Barney about my new angle, but I could not risk having my voice overheard once I left the shaft. For now, I would have to play it alone. Fifteen minutes later, I edged through the boards and made my way down the incline, picking my steps as carefully as possible to avoid any chance mishap that might alert Gorzik to my approach. The desert sand was soft under my boots, and I moved as noiselessly as I had hoped. The sun was almost up by the time I reached the crates behind the saloon. I could make them out clearly enough now, as well as the back door to the saloon. For a moment, I knelt behind the crates and listened. When I was satisfied that I had not been observed, I advanced again.

When I reached the back door, I was tempted to try the knob, but I feared that the rusty hinges might announce my presence prematurely and decided to wait exactly where I was until Juniper's handiwork was completed. After that, I had no idea what to expect. I could only hope that my decision-making would be sound enough and quick enough to locate Leigh and somehow get her away from Gorzik. I checked my watch again and waited. Another five minutes passed. I removed my backpack and set it on the ground. I took only my cell phone. I pulled my .38 and readied it, for I would harbor no qualms at all about drilling Gorzik on the spot. Only twice during my career had I ever had to shoot a man. Both times were warranted. I had not felt good on either occasion, but I knew that such actions sometimes came with the territory.

I placed my ear against the door and strained to hear anything inside, but I could pick up nothing. Where was Gorzik? Was he sitting down, listening for me as I was attempting to locate him? Was he near the front door as I suspected he might be, awaiting my arrival? Perhaps he was not even in the saloon. He might have moved to another location. Then again, maybe Juniper had been mistaken. I shook my head as these and other such thoughts ran through my mind. There was no way to be certain. I waited as patiently as I could, yet I was anything but patient. My heart was beating hard, I was sweating, and my mouth felt like cotton.

Again, I checked my watch. Juniper was five minutes late. Of course, he could not have been exact in his estimate of the time. Perhaps it had taken him longer than he'd thought to set his charge. Maybe he had experienced a problem of some kind.

The sun was up now, and the shadows were vanishing from the structures. I could discern objects in the distance, as well as those within the confines of Silver Butte. I began to feel uneasy.

I jerked violently as a red-tailed hawk flitted directly over my head and shrieked a discordant note. I took a deep breath and composed myself, wondering if it were the same creature I had seen during my first visit. It probably felt that I was the intruder here, infringing on its territory. Perhaps the bird was right. Perhaps no human belonged in this town of the past that had been forsaken so long ago.

It was then that I heard it—a distant muffled sound followed by a series of ground-shaking vibrations. I could feel the sand move beneath me. I could hear the rattle of loose boards as the saloon and adjoining buildings trembled. Suddenly I heard a roar from somewhere inside the saloon. It was a deep, guttural sound—definitely human yet somehow distorted by sheer terror. I could hear loud footsteps followed by cursing and grunting. I knew it had to be Gorzik, stomping about in a panic. The time was now!

I reached for the knob and turned it. The old door creaked loudly as I opened it and stepped inside. I glanced around but saw no sign of anyone. The storage area was empty. Hastily, I passed into the main room.

The bat-wing doors were swinging wildly, and I could see Gorzik out in the street, rushing about frenetically. I looked around, but I did not see Leigh anywhere.

"Leigh!" I called out to her, praying that she was still alive.

A dull murmur came from somewhere behind the bar.

Quickly, I moved toward the sound. I saw her feet and then her legs. She lay stretched out on the floor. Her ankles were bound with tape. As I maneuvered around the bar, I found her lying on her side, her eyes, mouth, and hands also bound with tape.

I set my .38 on the bar, removed my pocketknife, and immediately went to work removing the tape from her eyes. She blinked awkwardly for several seconds. Her eyes were wide with fear, yet she seemed to exude an expression of relief once she focused on me. It seemed to take me nearly a full minute to work the knife blade through the multiple strands of stubborn tape, but I made progress, freeing first her hands and then moving on to her ankles. I allowed her to remove the tape from her mouth herself.

When she was able to speak, she threw her arms around my neck and clutched me tightly in trembling arms. "Oh, John, I knew you'd come."

As I sliced through the final stretches of tape around her ankles, I explained to her where Barney was and how we were going to exit through the back door of the saloon.

"I . . . I don't think I can walk. I've been tied so long, my feet are numb."

I placed the cell phone in her hand and then began to massage her feet. "I might have to carry you, Leigh, but we have to get out of here fast. Gorzik could be back at any second."

I had barely finished my sentence when Leigh screamed.

"I am back, Hazard."

I turned and looked up to see Manny Gorzik standing on the opposite side of the bar, peering down at me. His massive face appeared unusually distorted as long strands of his curly black hair dangled loosely over his forehead, wet with perspiration. His huge lips were twisted in a combination of rage and panic, and his dark eyes bulged out like chunks of coal.

I reached for my .38, but Gorzik moved faster. He picked it up and tossed it over his shoulder.

"It's not going to be that easy," he said, grinning at me now with a baleful expression.

"Run, Leigh!" I shouted as I climbed to my feet and shot a right to Gorzik's jaw with everything I had. It landed cleanly and rocked Gorzik back on his heels. I vaulted onto the bar, balanced myself, and then leaped onto him. He raised his monstrous arms, deflecting my lunge, and the two of us hit the floor together and rolled around like combatants in a saloon brawl in a Western. Both of us climbed to our feet at the same time. Believing I had another clear shot at him, I threw a right. He caught my fist in the palm of his hand, pulled me toward him, and hefted me over his head as if I were a bag of laundry. The next thing I knew, I was being hurled across the room, where I landed on a table that shattered under my weight.

I lay where I was, dazed and in pain, for what must have been a full ten seconds before I felt the viselike grip of his hands on me again. He hoisted me to my feet, grabbed me by my shirt collar, and stared into my face as though he were a lion about to devour its prey. Before I had a chance to react, he head-butted me, knocking me off my feet again. When my head cleared, I realized I was sprawled on my back, staring at the ceiling. I wiped blood from my face with my shirtsleeve. Either my nose or my lip or both were oozing blood. I concluded that it must have been my nose, for it felt strange, numb. More than likely it was broken.

Somehow, I rolled to my side and got to my feet. Gorzik was approaching me once again, his long arms outstretched like those of an aggressive linebacker intent on bringing down a running back. I picked up a chair, fumbled with it, and dropped it. He laughed derisively and came closer. I managed to kick the chair into his path, and he stumbled over it. Outraged, he picked it up and shattered it across his thigh as if it were a Tinker Toy.

"I did hard time because of you, Hazard, and now I'm going to make you pay for it."

"You went to prison because you broke the law and

because you were a fool. Now, you've committed murder and kidnapping, and I'm going to see that you get the needle for it."

"I never murdered anybody, but you're going to be the first, you two-bit gumshoe."

"Then you'd better get to it, you overstuffed tub of lard. You're beginning to bore me."

He gritted his teeth so hard, I thought he was going to burst a blood vessel. He clenched his cantaloupe-sized fists in seething rage and suddenly lunged at me like a freight train that had jumped its track.

I sidestepped him, but just barely, for despite his damaged knee, he was remarkably quick for a man of his girth. I picked up one of the legs that had broken off the chair, turned, and swung it at him. I missed him by a good three inches. He ducked, weaved, and came at me again. This time, I waited until he was almost on me before I let him have it. The wood connected squarely with the top of his skull, shattering into small pieces. He staggered for a moment, and his eyes seemed to glaze over, but then he shook his head as if to clear it and came at me again.

My heart sank as I watched him recover from a blow that would have dropped most men, but Gorzik was no ordinary man. He was being fueled right now by a built-up hate that was exploding from within him like lava bursting from a volcano. Once again, he circled me, feigned a left punch, and then swung a roundhouse right that would have fractured my skull had he landed it.

Fortunately, I slipped under it and countered with two quick jabs to his midsection. They bounced off him innocuously, and he swatted me away with the back of one arm. I braced myself as he closed in again. I swung at him, but he ducked under my punch, stepped in, and wrapped his arms around me, lifting me off the floor as he held me in a stranglehold that took away my breath. He squeezed until my bones felt as if they were being crushed under the weight of a bulldozer. I could do nothing to extricate myself from his deathlike grip; I was completely helpless against his superior size and strength. I knew that I would black out in a matter of seconds, and a broken spine would follow soon after. My arms were free, but they seemed heavy, as though I could barely lift them. I strained with all I had, and somehow I was able to raise them enough to come level with his head. I mustered what little strength I had left and swung my open palms hard against his ears. He grunted in pain and, for a split second, loosened his grip. I slid through his arms and collapsed in a heap. I was in so much pain now, I knew I could not even stand. The next sensation I had was one of weightlessness as I realized that Gorzik was lifting me by my belt and the back of my shirt collar. He carried me in this fashion for a few steps and then suddenly flung me through the air. I closed my eyes and prayed that I would land on something soft. I did not. The sound of shattering glass was the last noise I heard as I sailed through a window of the saloon and landed on the boardwalk outside. I remembered trying to raise my head, but I could not. My skin felt strange, as though it had been pricked by needles. After that, I could see only black.

The first thing I saw when I came around was Leigh. She was kneeling over me, dabbing my face with something wet. Her hands were gentle as they moved solicitously across my skin.

"He's coming around," she announced.

My eyes seemed out of focus for a moment, but in time I could see her more clearly. She was smiling at me, relief in her face. She was easy on my eyes.

Barney and Juniper came into view.

"How are you feeling?" Barney asked.

"All right, I guess."

"You had a pretty good working-over."

I nodded.

"Feel like sitting up?"

"I suppose so."

"Maybe we shouldn't move him yet," Leigh cautioned.

"No, I think I'm okay. I just feel a little sore."

Barney and Juniper helped me to sit up. They turned me around so my back was against a wall. As far as I could tell, I was still on the boardwalk outside the saloon.

"Leigh . . . you're all right?"

"Yes, John. I called Barney, and he drove in immediately."

"Gorzik . . . where is he?"

Barney jerked a thumb over his shoulder.

I looked in the direction Barney indicated and saw Manny Gorzik sitting dejectedly at the end of the board-walk, his shoulder in a sling.

"Juniper shot him."

I glanced up at Juniper.

"I had no choice. I warned him to stop, but he kept comin'. Lucky you loaned me your .45. I had to put a round into him."

"That's good shooting."

"Not really. I missed the first two times." He grinned. "I patched him up the best I could, but he needs a doctor."

"Paramedics and the police are on the way," Leigh put in. "You could use some medical attention yourself."

"I do feel a little ragged."

"I gave you a once-over, son," Juniper said. "You've got a broken nose, at least two of your ribs are cracked or fractured, and you've got several cuts and bruises from goin' through that window. You're goin' to need some stitches, sure enough."

"What are you, a doctor?"

"I was a corpsman in Vietnam."

I nodded, once again amazed by the old prospector. "Well, there's one thing you missed. I do believe that I have a couple of loose teeth," I added as I gently touched my swollen lip.

Leigh leaned over and kissed me on the forehead. "I wish that could make everything better."

I managed a smile. "Believe me, it does. And I'm truly glad that you're safe and sound, Leigh."

"I wasn't hurt. I was home asleep in bed. I must have been drugged. The next thing I knew, I was here in this ghost town, bound and gagged. Gorzik never laid a hand on me. He was only interested in you. He talked sparingly, but I had a pretty good idea what was going on. I was just so afraid that he was going to kill you."

"He came pretty close."

"At least it's all over now."

"No, Leigh, it isn't. This case is still open. There's one final detail that requires my attention."

Chapter Ten

It was nearly quitting time when I walked into The Corner Florist. The shop was empty, and as I shut the door behind me, I flipped over the sign behind me to read CLOSED. A moment later, Myron Bendix emerged from the back room. He took one look at me, and his face turned two shades of red.

"Hello, Myron. It's nice to see you again."

"Mr. Hazard, how did you . . . I mean . . . why did you come back?"

"You seem more than a little surprised to see me. Did you think Manny Gorzik had killed me?"

"Manny . . . I don't know what you're talking about."

"Oh, really?" I strolled over to the counter and stood across from him. "It wasn't because Gorzik didn't try. In fact, he gave me a pretty good working-over—from my teeth to my ribs. He just couldn't quite finish the job."

Bendix stared at me incredulously. "I really don't know what you're talking about. You asked me before

158

about this Manny Gorzik, and I told you I didn't know him."

"It doesn't matter. Gorzik is no longer part of the equation."

"He's . . . dead?"

Ignoring him, I continued, "I really have to give you credit, Myron, for a masterful plan. All this time, I thought it was your brother who'd orchestrated this caper, but it was you."

He shook his head in denial.

"No, that won't do. I can see now how it all came together. I suspected poor Joe with his high IQ and his light fingers, but now I believe he was just someone who was duped by you in the same way I was."

"You don't know what you're saying."

"Oh, I think I do. Let me see if I can put it all together. Stop me if I make a wrong turn."

Myron eyed me narrowly as a nerve in his cheek began to twitch.

"Your brother, Joe, met Gorzik in prison. The warden indicated that the two of them hit it off pretty well. An odd relationship, if you ask me. Maybe it was because the two of them had something in common—a bum leg. I don't know, but prison sometimes makes for strange bedfellows. Joe learned about the grudge Gorzik held against me. That was when you found out about Gorzik— through conversations with and letters from your brother. Gorzik, in turn, learned about your rich uncle. Both he and Joe were released from prison within a month or so of each other. That's when you concocted the idea of doing away with your uncle and framing me for his murder. You knew that Gorzik would be a willing ally, since his hatred for me ran so deep."

"That's preposterous!"

I continued. "You found the washed-up actor, Lawrence Tracy, dragged him out of a bottle, and had him pose as your uncle. Because of your uncle's low public profile, you knew that no one had seen a picture of him in years, and it would be easy to pull off such a charade. You fed him some background material about your uncle and his works, and, with a little coaching, the rest was simple. Being a ham actor, Tracy took it from there and winged it. You even posed as your own brother, with a wig and some glasses . . . right down to the limp. My guess is that even Tracy knew you as your brother, Joe. It was a nice touch—and a little added insurance, in case something went wrong. If I had been arrested, I would have ID'd your brother, not you. The logical conclusion was to assume that it was your brother who was involved. After all, he already did time for trying to get his greedy hands on your uncle's fortune. Your record, on the other hand, was clean."

I paused. "Well, how am I doing so far?"

Myron shook his head, but his eyes narrowed as he stared at me malevolently.

"You then got my secretary out of town with that false alarm about her mother. Then it was my turn. You got rid of me with your trumped-up story about doing historical research in a ghost town." I shook my head. "I have to admit, it was an interesting invitation. It was so strange, I wouldn't have suspected it was a ruse in a million years. After that, with no one around my office, it was easy for you to gain entry, locate my backup .38, and use it on your uncle. I wonder what story you concocted to get him there. Or did you just use brute force? It doesn't really matter. I had no alibi, your uncle was shot in my office with my gun, and my fingerprints were all over it. Not bad. Not bad at all."

"Mr. Hazard, you have a very fertile imagination."

"The only thing you didn't count on was my ability to elude the police. That gave me time to do some digging." I stared at him for a long moment as he drummed his fingertips on the glass counter. "Of course, whenever an investigator starts to dig, he gets some dirt on his hands. I made things easier for you when I strolled into your shop the other day. You recognized me, of course, from our earlier encounter in that house in Santa Monica. You did a good acting job, pretending that you didn't know me. After I left, you called the police and told them I was looking for your brother, which was true enough. Then you killed two birds with one proverbial stone. You did away with Joe, and I became the primary suspect in his murder as well. In the process, you also became the sole heir to your uncle's estate—no splitting down the middle with your older brother." I paused to observe his reaction. "Well, have I managed to put things together reasonably accurately?"

His lips tightened as he sneered at me. "I'm going to call the police. You're still a murder suspect."

"Go ahead. Ask for Lieutenant Cornell in homicide."

Myron moved his hand toward his telephone but hesitated.

"You already started cleaning up your trail when you did away with Lawrence Tracy. Was it because he was planning to blackmail you, or did you simply want to eliminate all the witnesses?"

Suddenly Myron's hand snaked under the counter and came out holding a .22. He pointed it directly at me and grinned.

"Well, well, it appears as though I was right on the money."

"Not bad, Hazard. It's unfortunate you won't live long enough to explain it all to the police." Waving his gun at me, he said, "I suppose you're armed. Take it out slowly, and drop it to the floor."

I did as he directed, removing my .38 with two fingers and tossing it away.

"Your theory is pretty good. It's true that Tracy was trying to bleed me. Of course, he knew nothing about any of the murders. He was merely hired to play a part, but when he read the newspapers, he put two and two together and saw dollar signs. It didn't matter. I was planning to do away with him all along. It doesn't pay to have a lush around. Loose lips and all that."

"And your brother—how much did he really know?"

"My brother was a sniveling weakling. He had no

problem with trying to steal from our uncle on paper, but when it came to murder, he was a no-show."

"He knew nothing about your plan?"

"Not until he read about our uncle's death in the newspapers. That was when he confronted me about it. We quarreled. He thought the police would suspect him of the crime." He chuckled. "He was right. That was the whole point. I knew, in time, he would break, so I had to get rid of him. Of course, when you came by inquiring about him, I had the opportunity to play you for a patsy twice over."

"What about Henry Waller?"

"Who?"

"The man I found in the closet in that house in Santa Monica."

He waved his gun matter-of-factly. "Oh, that was an accident. The house was supposed to be unoccupied for the season. He was a caretaker or something of the kind. He just wandered in at the wrong time. He almost ruined everything."

"Four murders, including your own brother and your uncle." I shook my head in disgust. "I hope it was worth it."

"It will be. My uncle's estate is estimated at over two million."

"And what would you have done about Gorzik? Did you have plans for him as well?"

He grinned. "An ex-con loser with a hatred so deep it blinded his reason. He was useful but expendable. It would've been easy to eliminate him. Luckily, you took care of him for me. Actually, I'm a little surprised. I didn't think you had a chance against him."

"I guess I got lucky."

"Funny, you don't look lucky from where I'm standing."

"I suppose I'm slated to become victim number five on your list."

"Your count is correct."

"What's your cover story?"

He shrugged. "Simple. You came here and threatened me. I tried to call the police. You pulled your gun. I fired first."

"Not too shabby . . . except for a couple of minor details."

"Like what?"

"Like Manny Gorzik, for one thing."

"What about him?"

"He's alive."

Myron's grin disappeared. "You said—"

"I didn't say he was dead. You just drew the wrong conclusion. Gorzik is in police custody right now, and he's probably copping a plea to save what's left of the life he has."

Myron's eyes flitted back and forth as he was processing my remarks.

"You're through. Washed-up. You'll get the needle."

Myron's tongue shot out nervously as he licked his lips. "It's Gorzik's word against mine."

I shook my head. "It's also my word against yours. Don't forget, I just heard you confess to four murders."

"But you won't be around, Hazard."

"I think I will, Myron," I replied.

He stared at me with an odd expression. He started to speak, but no words came from his mouth.

"Drop the gun, Mr. Bendix."

Myron turned suddenly and faced Pete Cornell, who was standing in the doorway of the back room. At six-three, 230 pounds, and ramrod straight, Cornell looked imposing with his police special trained on Myron. Myron hesitated, looking at Cornell and then again at me.

"Did you hear anything interesting, Pete?" I asked.

"I heard enough."

At that moment, two uniformed officers entered through the front door, their weapons also trained on Myron.

Immediately, Myron placed his .22 on the counter and raised his hands.

"Cuff him!" Cornell instructed.

One of the officers frisked Myron and placed handcuffs on him while the other picked up his .22 and read him his rights.

Myron said nothing. He merely hung his head as he was removed from the shop.

I suddenly felt like wet paper, and I had to lean over the counter to stand up.

I felt Cornell's hand under my arm, half holding me up.

"That's it, fella. You need some bed rest."

I nodded.

"You've done enough. You've proved your case. Let the regulars take it from here."

"Aren't you going to take me downtown?"

"No. I know where to find you."

I glanced at him and smiled. "Are you sure?"

He smiled back. "Don't leave town."

"Oh, and I was planning on returning to Silver Butte."

Chapter Eleven

The alarm clock jarred me out of an uneasy sleep. I turned it off and shut my eyes again. Twenty minutes later, I got to my feet. My ribs felt as if somebody had buried a spike in them—a dull, rusty spike. I grunted deeply as I took pigeon steps toward the bathroom.

The light over my mirror seemed more glaring than usual as I surveyed what was left of my body. My nose was broken and sensitive to my touch. Both of my eyes were black, and my face was swollen. Bandages covered my forearms, where I'd needed twelve stitches in one and ten in the other. I looked like something that had washed up on the shore.

After I cleaned up, I stumbled around in the kitchen and managed to brew some coffee.

The doorbell rang, and I groaned as I headed for the door. I opened it to find Pete Cornell standing on my porch with my newspaper in his hand.

"Hello, Pete."

"Good morning, John. How are you feeling?"

"Sore, tired, old."

"So, what else is new?"

He stepped inside and handed me the paper. "You've been getting some pretty good press."

"Oh? I wish I could say that that makes me feel better."

"I've been trying to reach you, but your phone's been busy."

"I took it off the hook. Too many calls. Reporters, newsmen . . . I've had it. Some radio shock-jock called and wanted to interview me on the air. A screenwriter from Burbank wanted to do a script about me. Enough is enough."

He chuckled. "Maybe they'll do a TV series about you. I can see the intro now—you leaping through a plate-glass window, your .38 blazing."

"Uh-huh. What are you doing here anyway? Don't you have some bank robbers to chase?"

"Evelyn took the kids to her mother's for a few days. I thought I'd come over for a cup of coffee."

"The coffee's on, but I haven't managed to make breakfast yet. Have you eaten?"

"No."

"You can join me."

"Thanks. I'll fix it. In the meantime, you can read about how wonderful you are."

I sat down at the table and found the feature article, the cornerstone of which was Richard Armitage.

"How do you like your eggs?" he asked as he opened the refrigerator.

"Soft. No toast for me."

"Your teeth still bothering you?"

"Yeah. No steaks or chops for a while."

"What exactly did your dentist do?"

"He used an adhesive to join my loose teeth to the adjoining ones—a kind of splint, he called it."

"Sounds awful."

"It is."

"You still going to the same dentist—the one who was in your dorm in college?"

"Yeah. Marvin."

"I heard he's good."

"He is."

"I don't see any orange juice."

"Don't have any."

"Sunny California and no orange juice?"

"Black coffee."

As Pete started breakfast, I begin to skim through the article. The media were having a field day with all the murders, but from what I gathered, they were finally getting most of the details straight. In this edition, there was some interesting background material on Myron Bendix. It seemed that a reporter had tracked down his ex-wife in Boston. During his interview with her, she'd painted a pretty bleak picture of Myron, accusing him of concealing assets from her during their marriage and refusing to pay alimony and child support after their divorce. She also suggested that he was guilty of income tax evasion. I figured that Myron was in about as much trouble as a person could be in.

There was a picture of Manny Gorzik, his head hanging low as he was being led away by deputies. Next to it was an old picture of him wearing some strange wrestling costume and leaping through the air.

There was a picture of me and a long column detailing my involvement in the apprehension of Gorzik and Myron Bendix. There were a few gaps here and there, but except for an occasional misquote, I could not complain about the coverage.

When Pete placed my eggs on the table, I threw down the paper.

"I just thought I'd let you know that Manny Gorzik is cooperating completely. His spirit seems to be broken. I don't think he even cares about you anymore."

"What about Myron Bendix?"

"A tale of two cities. He's doing his impression of a clam at low tide."

"I'm not surprised."

"By the way, we learned that Myron Bendix actually took acting lessons some time back."

"That's how he met Tracy?"

"That's right." He poured the coffee and then sat down opposite me. "He also learned about makeup and wardrobe. We found several interesting articles in his closet, including an assortment of wigs."

I raised an eyebrow. "Including a blond one?"

"Yep."

We ate in silence for the next few minutes. Then Pete added, "One strange thing. Gorzik still claims that he didn't kill anyone. He claims that Bendix did all the murders."

I took a swallow of coffee as I considered his remark. "For my money, he's telling the truth."

"How's that?" he asked, surprised.

"When Gorzik had me cornered in that saloon back in Silver Butte, I called him a murderer. He flatly denied it. At that point in time, there was no reason for him to lie. As far as he was concerned, I wasn't going to walk out of there. Plus, Myron all but admitted all the murders to me in his shop."

"Hmm. There's some logic to that, I suppose, but Gorzik certainly had to be aware of what Myron had planned for his uncle, and that's conspiracy."

"I imagine so. I'll let the courts worry about that."

"Yeah." He filled our cups again, and we finished the rest of the meal.

The food helped, and my head felt better.

"I'll keep you posted as the rest of this case unravels," Pete offered.

"I'd appreciate it."

"Well, I'd better get moving. When you're feeling up to it, we can have lunch. Let me know."

"Okay, Pete. I will. Thanks for dropping by."

After Pete left, I maneuvered myself into a dress

shirt, trousers, and a sports coat, and then drove to the office.

Leigh was surprised to see me walk in. She rose from behind her desk, hastened over, and greeted me with a gentle hug. She looked good in a close-fitting, sleeveless pink dress, and she smelled of lavender as she warmly kissed me on the cheek.

"John, you shouldn't be here. You know what the doctor said," she stated, concern written on her face.

"I know, but I've been in hiding for a long time now. It just doesn't feel right being cooped up any longer. Besides, there's paperwork to catch up on, and I have to pay the bills."

"Oh, that can wait."

I shrugged.

"How are your ribs?"

"Rocky—especially when I'm in bed. I spent most of the night in my recliner."

She shook her head sympathetically. "Your face is still swollen. You look like you've been through the proverbial wringer."

"Thanks for the compliment. Look at it this way— Manny Gorzik just added some character to my face."

She shook her head at my reference to her own earlier injury—at my hands. "The phone has been ringing off the hook—reporters, friends, well-wishers. I've filled them in as much as I could. I told them you'll call them back when you're up to it."

"That's fine."

"I'll get you some coffee," she said with a smile.

"Thanks," I replied as I walked into my office again for the first time in what seemed like forever. I eased gingerly into my armchair and wondered if it would be worth getting out of it for the rest of the day.

A minute later Leigh entered with my cup and the newspaper. "Have you seen the latest edition?" she asked excitedly.

"I skimmed through it."

"It's a wonderful article. It explains how you solved the Richard Armitage murder even while you were a fugitive. I'm so proud of you. Did you see the picture of you on page three? It's very flattering!"

I groaned. "It's a good thing they didn't take a picture of me the way I look now."

"Oh, you'll be back to normal in a few days. A broken nose isn't all that bad. I even broke mine once when I was in junior high."

"That makes me feel better."

She smirked.

I sipped my coffee and glanced at the paperwork that lay ahead of me.

"This publicity should bring in some heavy-duty clients," she said dreamily.

"I wanted to talk to you about that. I've been giving some serious consideration to retiring."

"You said you wanted to work three more years."

"I feel older now."

"You can't mean that, can you?" she asked sadly.

"Actually, I do mean it."

"You'll get over that. Look at me—I got over being kidnapped."

I nodded. "I'm glad about that, Leigh. Maybe they should have taken *your* picture."

"They did."

"How's that?"

She smiled. "A photographer took my picture this morning. It should be in tomorrow's paper."

"Oh, so that's why you look so alluring today."

She blushed.

"I suppose the magazines and the tabloids will be next. Then some producer will offer you a part in a movie. If I do stay on, I'll have to hire a new secretary anyway."

"Oh, please. Just give me the darn raise, John." She smirked again.

I nodded, then started in on my paperwork, hoping to put Manny Gorzik and Myron Bendix out of my mind until their arraignment. Leigh was in a solicitous mood and seemed to find a reason to come in every twenty minutes or so to refill my cup or adjust the blinds. Along about noon, she popped in again.

"Do you have time to see someone without an appointment?"

I looked up and saw Charlie Doyle standing in the doorway.

Leigh giggled.

"Hiya, partner," Charlie said, grinning broadly.

I levered myself out of my chair and walked around the desk to greet him.

"I've been reading up on you. It's too bad you didn't get this much publicity while I was still with the agency. It might have improved our clientele—and our payroll."

I smiled at him. "Charlie, it's great to see you!"

He shook my hand firmly and stood eye to eye with me. Suddenly his big Scottish grin disappeared, and genuine concern covered his face. "I heard you had it pretty rough, lad."

I nodded.

"How are you, really?"

"Oh, a little worn out, but I'm all right."

"Good."

In a moment, Leigh brought in a cup of coffee for Charlie. We both sat down and looked at each other. Charlie ran a hand through his thick patch of gray hair and settled back against the thickly padded armchair. He took a sip of coffee and smiled. "Leigh still makes a good cup of java."

"That she does."

"I'm sorry I wasn't around to lend a hand when you needed it."

I shrugged. "It all worked out."

"Leigh doesn't appear to be any the worse for wear."

"No, she's a strong girl. She handled everything as well as anybody could have, and she was there for me all the way. She's a professional."

"Manny Gorzik turned out to be a bad penny."

"I don't think he'll be turning up anymore after this."

"I'll drink to that."

"How are Alice and the kids?"

"Great. Everybody's happy and in good health."

"When did you get into town?"

"Last night."

"Where are you staying?"

"With Mary and Frank. We brought the grandkids back, and we'll be in LA for about a week. We'd like to have you over to dinner."

"Sounds good."

He rubbed his knee and grimaced a bit.

"Your RA acting up again?"

"It only hurts when I sit still and when I move."

I smiled.

He eyed me narrowly. "And what about you?"

"Oh, the ribs still hurt and—"

"I don't mean your injuries."

"What do you mean?"

"Well, Leigh is under the impression that you're going to close the agency."

"I'm seriously considering it."

"You've been roughed up before. You were even shot once."

"Oh, it's not only that. I guess I've just had it. I've seen enough of the grifters and the opportunists, the gutters and the back alleys. I'm tired of dealing with lowlifes. You know what I mean. You've been there yourself."

"I know."

I could not quite read his expression. "What is it you want to say?"

"Nothing. You have every right to call it a day."

"But?"

He shrugged. "Our profession is like any other. Some of us are just looking to turn a fast buck and don't care how. Others are here for the right reason. You're that kind of investigator. You're good for this job."

"I'm tired."

"We all get tired, and we all get fed up, but you've made a difference. You've helped when help was needed, and you did it the right way."

I considered his comments as I took a swallow of my coffee.

"When you decide to leave, do it on your own terms, not because somebody like Manny Gorzik ended your career. It will leave you with a bad taste in your mouth."

I watched him as he stood up and tried to straighten out his stiff knee.

"Well, I'll leave you to your paperwork. I'll be in touch about that dinner as soon as Alice works out the details."

We shook hands again, and he walked out of the office, favoring his left leg.

For the next half hour or so, I tried to concentrate on my work, but I was finding it more difficult. I was relieved when Leigh buzzed me and announced excitedly that Juniper was on the phone. I picked up the receiver and was both surprised and delighted to hear from the old prospector.

"Son, how are you gettin' on?" he asked, a peppery edge in his voice.

"I'm recovering nicely, thanks to you."

"Oh, it was nothin'," he replied modestly.

"Where are you calling from?"

"Silver Butte."

"But how?"

"I got me one of those cell phones."

"Really?"

"That's right. A man has to modernize sometimes."

I chuckled.

"The reason I called was to give you the good news. Remember that little makeshift earthquake that we created?"

"I'll never forget it. It did the trick in saving Leigh's life."

"Well, it just so happened that the explosion opened up a new vein. It's pure silver—a foot wide for who knows how long. I'm finally a rich man."

I laughed out loud. "Congratulations! It couldn't have happened to a more deserving person."

I heard his laughter ring in my ear.

"But, Juniper, who owns the land that Silver Butte is on?"

"Why, I do."

"You do?"

"That's right. I've owned it for the last ten years.

It was considered pretty useless, remember. I got it cheap."

"But you never said anything to me when I was there. Technically, I was trespassing on your property."

"That doesn't bother me. There's always somebody driftin' through ghost towns. They're part of our history. The only thing I was interested in when I bought the land was silver."

"Well, what do you plan to do, now that you're a tycoon?"

"Shucks, I may just renovate the entire town—a new saloon with brass doorknobs and spittoons. A brand-new hotel would be nice. I could turn Silver Butte into one of those tourist attractions for folks who want to visit the old West as it once existed."

"Sounds interesting. You can book me into that hotel as your first guest."

"I'll count on it, son. You get well now, and we'll stay in touch."

"So long, Juniper. Give my regards to Harry Truman."

As I hung up the receiver, I could not help but grin broadly, absolutely elated over Juniper's success. I called in Leigh and shared the news with her. She, too, was excited. We chatted about him for a while until the telephone rang again. Leigh answered it. She turned to me and announced, "It's Margie at the diner. She says Barney has a fresh batch of chili if you're up for it."

"I suppose I could eat chili, even with loose teeth. Tell her yes. I'll be there in an hour or so."

Leigh delivered the message and hung up.

"Why don't you lock up and come along?" I suggested.

She shook her head. "No, you go ahead. I have a few errands to run."

"Oh?"

"I'm going to do some shopping. I thought I'd have you over to dinner tonight—that is, if you feel up to it."

"What are you having?"

"I was going to fix your favorite—pot roast—but I'm not sure you could chew it."

"You're right."

"How about some broiled salmon?"

"I could eat that, and I love salmon."

"Good. Shall we say seven o'clock?"

I nodded.

She smiled, turned on her heel, and left the office.

I worked for a while longer. Then my ribs started to bother me again. I took a few shallow breaths, swiveled my chair around, and stared out the window. As I watched the traffic moving mechanically back and forth, I wondered about what Charlie had said.

A few minutes later, I heard the outer door open, and I turned around. A middle-aged couple stood in the waiting room. I left my desk and went out to meet them.

"I'm sorry, but the office is officially closed today. I'm a little under the weather, and I'm not taking on any cases at this time."

"We know," the man replied. "We read about you in

the newspaper, Mr. Hazard. We're sorry to hear about your injuries."

They were distinguished looking, well dressed, probably in their early fifties. The man had gray hair and was thin, almost frail. The woman was short and wore her hair in a tight bun. They both appeared to be under a great strain.

"Yes, I've been through quite a bit lately."

The man shifted his weight uneasily from one foot to the other. "We don't know anyone here in Los Angeles. We only arrived yesterday, but we were impressed with what we read about you."

"Where are you from?"

"Akron, Ohio."

"We're looking for our daughter," the woman put in. "We haven't heard from her in weeks. She came out here a little over a month ago, looking for work."

"What kind of work?"

"She wants to be an actress," the woman returned, forcing a smile. "She's only nineteen, but you know how young people can be."

I nodded.

"She was in constant contact with us for the first two weeks, as she'd promised she would be, but after that, well . . ." The woman started to break down.

Her husband placed his arm around her shoulders and hung his head.

"Why don't you come into my office?"

I seated them in front of my desk and poured them

some coffee. That seemed to settle the woman a little. When she was more composed, she removed a snapshot from her purse and placed it on my desk.

I examined it closely. The girl in the picture was very pretty—blond, a nice smile. She looked like so many others her age who headed for the big city to make their mark. An exceptional few made it, but most of them did not. For most, the glitz and glamour proved unattainable, and they returned home. Some never did. It was an old story.

I listened to the mother speak lovingly of her daughter's achievements—the high school glee and drama clubs, the voice lessons, the college theater courses. I sympathized with the parents. They had that look—the look I had seen so many times before—the furrowed brows, the red eyes, the thin lips. I sat back and listened closely, letting them pour out their souls. Maybe my ribs were not that bad after all. I imagined I could live with them. I did not know if these parents could live with their fears and concerns.

I listened.